The Hymns of Prudentius

Aurelius Clemens Prudentius

Contents

THE HYMNS OF PRUDENTIUS

BY

Aurelius Clemens Prudentius

PRAEFATIO

Per quinquennia iam decem,
ni fallor, fuimus: septimus insuper
annum cardo rotat, dum fruimur sole volubili.
　Instat terminus et diem
vicinum senio iam Deus adplicat.　　　　　　　5
Quid nos utile tanti spatio temporis egimus?
　Aetas prima crepantibus
flevit sub ferulis: mox docuit toga
infectum vitiis falsa loqui, non sine crimine.
　Tum lasciva protervitas,　　　　　　　　10
et luxus petulans (heu pudet ac piget)
foedavit iuvenem nequitiae sordibus ac luto.
　Exin iurgia turbidos
armarunt animos et male pertinax
vincendi studium subiacuit casibus asperis.　　15
　Bis legum moderamine
frenos nobilium reximus urbium,
ius civile bonis reddidimus, terruimus reos.
　Tandem militiae gradu
evectum pietas principis extulit　　　　　　20
adsumptum propius stare iubens ordine proximo.
　Haec dum vita volans agit,
inrepsit subito canities seni
oblitum veteris me Saliae consulis arguens:

ex quo prima dies mihi   25
quam multas hiemes volverit et rosas
pratis post glaciem reddiderit, nix capitis probat.
  Numquid talia proderunt
carnis post obitum vel bona vel mala,
cum iam, quidquid id est, quod fueram, mors aboleverit?   30
  Dicendum mihi; Quisquis es,
mundum, quem coluit, mens tua perdidit:
non sunt illa Dei, quae studuit, cuius habeberis.
  Atqui fine sub ultimo
peccatrix anima stultitiam exuat: 35
saltem voce Deum concelebret, si meritis nequit:
  hymnis continuet dies,
nec nox ulla vacet, quin Dominum canat:
pugnet contra hereses, catholicam discutiat fidem,
  conculcet sacra gentium,   40
labem, Roma, tuis inferat idolis,
carmen martyribus devoveat, laudet apostolos.
  Haec dum scribo vel eloquor,
vinclis o utinam corporis emicem
liber, quo tulerit lingua sono mobilis ultimo.   45

PREFACE

Full fifty years my span of life hath run,
Unless I err, and seven revolving years
Have further sped while I the sun enjoy.
Yet now the end draws nigh, and by God's will
Old age's bound is reached: how have I spent
And with what fruit so wide a tract of days?
I wept in boyhood 'neath the sounding rod:
Youth's toga donned, the rhetorician's arts
I plied and with deceitful pleadings sinned:
Anon a wanton life and dalliance gross
(Alas! the recollection stings to shame!)
Fouled and polluted manhood's opening bloom:
And then the forum's strife my restless wits
Enthralled, and the keen lust of victory
Drove me to many a bitterness and fall.
Twice held I in fair cities of renown
The reins of office, and administered
To good men justice and to guilty doom.
At length the Emperor's will beneficent
Exalted me to military power
And to the rank that borders on the throne.
The years are speeding onward, and gray hairs
Of old have mantled o'er my brows
And Salia's consulship from memory dies.

What frost-bound winters since that natal year
Have fled, what vernal suns reclothed
The meads with roses,--this white crown declares.
Yet what avail the prizes or the blows
Of fortune, when the body's spark is quenched
And death annuls whatever state I held?
This sentence I must hear: "Whate'er thou art,
Thy mind hath lost the world it loved: not God's
The things thou soughtest, Whose thou now shalt be."
Yet now, ere hence I pass, my sinning soul
Shall doff its folly and shall praise my Lord
If not by deeds, at least with humble lips.
Let each day link itself with grateful hymns
And every night re-echo songs of God:
Yea, be it mine to fight all heresies,
Unfold the meanings of the Catholic faith,
Trample on Gentile rites, thy gods, O Rome,
Dethrone, the Martyrs laud, th' Apostles sing.
O while such themes my pen and tongue employ,
May death strike off these fetters of the flesh
And bear me whither my last breath shall rise!

I. HYMNUS AD GALLI CANTUM

Ales diei nuntius
lucem propinquam praecinit;
nos excitator mentium
iam Christus ad vitam vocat.

Auferte, clamat, lectulos   5
aegros, soporos, desides:
castique recti ac sobrii
vigilate, iam sum proximus.

Post solis ortum fulgidi
serum est cubile spernere,   10
ni parte noctis addita
tempus labori adieceris.

Vox ista, qua strepunt aves
stantes sub ipso culmine
paulo ante quam lux emicet,   15
nostri figura est iudicis.

Tectos tenebris horridis
stratisque opertos segnibus
suadet quietem linquere

iam iamque venturo die.   20

Ut, cum coruscis flatibus
aurora caelum sparserit,
omnes labore exercitos
confirmet ad spem luminis.

Hic somnus ad tempus datus   25
est forma mortis perpetis,
peccata ceu nox horrida
cogunt iacere ac stertere.

Sed vox ab alto culmine
Christi docentis praemonet,   30
adesse iam lucem prope,
ne mens sopori serviat:

Ne somnus usque ad terminos
vitae socordis opprimat
pectus sepultum crimine   35
et lucis oblitum suae.

Ferunt vagantes daemonas
laetos tenebris noctium,
gallo canente exterritos
sparsim timere et cedere.   40

Invisa nam vicinitas
lucis, salutis, numinis
rupto tenebrarum situ
noctis fugat satellites.

Hoc esse signum praescii   45
norunt repromissae spei,
qua nos soporis liberi
speramus adventum Dei.

Quae vis sit huius alitis,
salvator ostendit Petro,   50
ter antequam gallus canat
sese negandum praedicans.

Fit namque peccatum prius,
quam praeco lucis proximae
inlustret humanum genus   55
finemque peccandi ferat.

Flevit negator denique
ex ore prolapsum nefas,
cum mens maneret innocens,
animusque servaret fidem.   60

Nec tale quidquam postea
linguae locutus lubrico est,
cantuque galli cognito
peccare iustus destitit.

Inde est quod omnes credimus,   65
illo quietis tempore
quo gallus exsultans canit
Christum redisse ex inferis.

Tunc mortis oppressus vigor,
tunc lex subacta est tartari,   70
tunc vis diei fortior

noctem coegit cedere.

Iam iam quiescant inproba,
iam culpa furva obdormiat,
iam noxa letalis suum   75
perpessa somnum marceat.

Vigil vicissim spiritus
quodcumque restat temporis,
dum meta noctis clauditur,
stans ac laborans excubet.   80

Iesum ciamus vocibus
flentes, precantes, sobrii:
intenta supplicatio
dormire cor mundum vetat.

Sat convolutis artubus   85
sensum profunda oblivio
pressit, gravavit, obruit
vanis vagantem somniis.

Sunt nempe falsa et frivola,
quae mundiali gloria   90
ceu dormientes egimus:
vigilemus, hic est veritas.

Aurum, voluptas, gaudium,
opes, honores, prospera,
quaecumque nos inflant mala,   95
fit mane, nil sunt omnia.

Tu, Christe, somnum dissice,

tu rumpe noctis vincula,
tu solve peccatum vetus
novumque lumen ingere.   100

I. HYMN AT COCK-CROW

Awake! the shining day is born!
The herald cock proclaims the morn:
And Christ, the soul's Awakener, cries,
Bidding us back to life arise.

Away the sluggard's bed! away
The slumber of the soul's decay!
Ye chaste and just and temperate,
Watch! I am standing at the gate.

After the sun hath risen red
'Tis late for men to scorn their bed,
Unless a portion of the night
They seize for labours of the light.

Mark ye, what time the dawn draws nigh,
How 'neath the eaves the swallows cry?
Know that by true similitude
Their notes our Judge's voice prelude.

When hid by shades of dark malign
On beds of softness we recline,
They call us forth with music clear
Warning us that the day is near.

When breezes bright of orient morn
With rosy hues the heavens adorn,
They cheer with hope of gladdening light
The hearts that spend in toil their might.

Though sleep be but a passing guest
'Tis type of death's perpetual rest:
Our sins are as a ghastly night,
And seal with slumbers deep our sight.

But from the wide roof of the sky
Christ's voice peals forth with urgent cry,
Calling our sleep-bound hearts to rise
And greet the dawn with wakeful eyes.

He bids us fear lest sensual ease
Unto life's end the spirit seize
And in the tomb of shame us bind,
Till we are to the true light blind.

'Tis said that baleful spirits roam
Abroad beneath the dark's vast dome;
But, when the cock crows, take their flight
Sudden dispersed in sore affright.

For the foul votaries of the night
Abhor the coming of the light,
And shamed before salvation's grace
The hosts of darkness hide their face.

They know the cock doth prophesy
Of Hope's long-promised morning sky,

When comes the Majesty Divine
Upon awakened worlds to shine.

The Lord to Peter once foretold
What meaning that shrill strain should hold,
How he before cock-crow would lie
And thrice his Master dear deny.

For 'tis a law that sin is done
Before the herald of the sun
To humankind the dawn proclaims
And with his cry the sinner shames.

Then wept he bitter tears aghast
That from his lips the words had passed,
Though guileless he his soul possessed
And faith still reigned within his breast.

Nor ever reckless word he said
Thereafter, by his tongue betrayed,
But at the cock's familiar cry
Humbled he turned from vanity.

Therefore it is we hold to-day
That, as the world in stillness lay,
What hour the cock doth greet the skies,
Christ from deep Hades did arise.

Lo! then the bands of death were burst,
Shattered the sway of hell accurst:
Then did the Day's superior might
Swiftly dispel the hosts of Night.

Now let base deeds to silence fall,
Black thoughts be stilled beyond recall:
Now let sin's opiate spell retire
To that deep sleep it doth inspire.

For all the hours that still remain
Until the dark his goal attain,
Alert for duty's stern command
Let every soul a sentry stand.

With sober prayer on Jesus call;
Let tears with our strong crying fall;
Sleep cannot on the pure soul steal
That supplicates with fervent zeal.

Too long did dull oblivion cloud
Our motions and our senses shroud:
Lulled by her numbing touch, we stray
In dreamland's ineffectual way.

Bound by the dazzling world's soft chain
'Tis false and fleeting gauds we gain,
Like those who in deep slumbers lie:--
Let us awake! the truth is nigh.

Gold, honours, pleasure, wealth and ease,
And all the joys that mortals please,
Joys with a fatal glamour fraught--
When morning comes, lo! all are nought.
But thou, O Christ, put sleep to flight
And break the iron bands of night,
Free us from burden of past sin
And shed Thy morning rays within.

II. HYMNUS MATUTINUS

Nox et tenebrae et nubila,
confusa mundi et turbida,
lux intrat, albescit polus,
Christus venit, discedite.

Caligo terrae scinditur   5
percussa solis spiculo,
rebusque iam color redit
vultu nitentis sideris.

Sic nostra mox obscuritas
fraudisque pectus conscium   10
ruptis retectum nubibus
regnante pallescit Deo.

Tunc non licebit claudere
quod quisque fuscum cogitat,
sed mane clarescent novo   15
secreta mentis prodita.

Fur ante lucem squalido
inpune peccat tempore,
sed lux dolis contraria
latere furtum non sinit.   20

Versuta fraus et callida
amat tenebris obtegi,
aptamque noctem turpibus
adulter occultus fovet.

Sol ecce surgit igneus,   25
piget, pudescit, paenitet,
nec teste quisquam lumine
peccare constanter potest.

Quis mane sumptis nequiter
non erubescit poculis,   30
cum fit libido temperans
castumque nugator sapit?

Nunc, nunc severum vivitur,
nunc nemo tentat ludicrum,
inepta nunc omnes sua   35
vultu colorant serio.

Haec hora cunctis utilis,
qua quisque, quod studet, gerat,
miles, togatus, navita,
opifex, arator, institor.   40

Illum forensis gloria,
hunc triste raptat classicum,
mercator hinc ac rusticus
avara suspirant lucra.

At nos lucelli ac faenoris   45
fandique prorsus nescii,
nec arte fortes bellica,

te, Christe, solum novimus.

Te mente pura et simplici,
te voce, te cantu pio   50
rogare curvato genu
flendo et canendo discimus.

His nos lucramur quaestibus,
hac arte tantum vivimus,
haec inchoamus munera,   55
cum sol resurgens emicat.

Intende nostris sensibus,
vitamque totam dispice,
sunt multa fucis inlita,
quae luce purgentur tua.   60

Durare nos tales iube,
quales, remotis sordibus
nitere pridem iusseras,
Iordane tinctos flumine.

Quodcumque nox mundi dehinc   65
infecit atris nubibus,
tu, rex Eoi sideris,
vultu sereno inlumina.

Tu sancte, qui taetram picem
candore tingis lacteo   70
ebenoque crystallum facis,
delicta terge livida.

Sub nocte Iacob caerula
luctator audax angeli,
eo usque dum lux surgeret,   75
sudavit inpar praelium.

Sed cum iubar claresceret,
lapsante claudus poplite
femurque victus debile
culpae vigorem perdidit.   80

Nutabat inguen saucium,
quae corporis pars vilior
longeque sub cordis loco
diram fovet libidinem.

Hae nos docent imagines,   85
hominem tenebris obsitum,
si forte non cedat Deo,
vires rebellis perdere.

Erit tamen beatior,
intemperans membrum cui   90
luctando claudum et tabidum
dies oborta invenerit.

Tandem facessat caecitas,
quae nosmet in praeceps diu
lapsos sinistris gressibus   95
errore traxit devio.

Haec lux serenum conferat
purosque nos praestet sibi:
nihil loquamur subdolum,

volvamus obscurum nihil.   100

  Sic tota decurrat dies,
ne lingua mendax, ne manus,
oculive peccent lubrici,
ne noxa corpus inquinet.

  Speculator adstat desuper,   105
qui nos diebus omnibus
actusque nostros prospicit
a luce prima in vesperum.

  Hic testis, hic est arbiter,
his intuetur quidquid est,   110
humana quod mens concipit;
hunc nemo fallit iudicem.

II. MORNING HYMN

Ye clouds and darkness, hosts of night
That breed confusion and affright,
Begone! o'erhead the dawn shines clear,
The light breaks in and Christ is here.

Earth's gloom flees broken and dispersed,
By the sun's piercing shafts coerced:
The daystar's eyes rain influence bright
And colours glimmer back to sight.

So shall our guilty midnight fade,
The sin-stained heart's gross dusky shade:
So shall the King's All-radiant Face
Sudden unveil our deep disgrace.

No longer then may we disguise
Our dark intents from those clear eyes:
Yea, at the dayspring's advent blest
Our inmost thoughts will stand confest.

The thief his hidden traffic plies
Unmarked before the dawn doth rise:
But light, the foe of guile concealed,
Lets no ill craft lie unrevealed.

Fraud and Deceit love only night,
Their wiles they practise out of sight;
Curtained by dark, Adultery too
Doth his foul treachery pursue,

But slinks abashed and shamed away
Soon as the sun rekindles day,
For none can damning light resist
And 'neath its rays in sin persist.

Who doth not blush o'ertook by morn
And his long night's carousal scorn?
For day subdues the lustful soul,
And doth all foul desires control.

Now each to earnest life awakes,
Now each his wanton sport forsakes;
Now foolish things are put away
And gravity resumes her sway.

It is the hour for duty's deeds,
The path to which our labour leads,
Be it the forum, army, sea,
The mart or field or factory.

One seeks the plaudits of the bar,
One the stern trumpet calls to war:
Those bent on trade and husbandry
At greed's behest for lucre sigh.

Mine is no rhetorician's fame,
No petty usury I claim;
Nor am I skilled to face the foe:

'Tis Thou, O Christ, alone I know.

Yea, I have learnt to wait on Thee
With heart and lips of purity,
Humbly my knees in prayer to bend,
And tears with songs of praise to blend.

These are the gains I hold in view
And these the arts that I pursue:
These are the offices I ply
When the bright sun mounts up the sky.

Prove Thou my heart, my every thought,
Search into all that I have wrought:
Though I be stained with blots within,
Thy quickening rays shall purge my sin.

O may I ever spotless be
As when my stains were cleansed by Thee,
Who bad'st me 'neath the Jordan's wave
Of yore my soiled spirit lave.

If e'er since then the world's gross night
Hath cast its curtain o'er my sight,
Dispel the cloud, O King of grace,
Star of the East! with thy pure face.

Since Thou canst change, O holy Light,
The blackest hue to milky white,
Ebon to clearness crystalline,
Wash my foul stains and make me clean.

'Twas 'neath the lonely star-blue night
That Jacob waged the unequal fight,
Stoutly he wrestled with the Man
In darkness, till the day began.

And when the sun rose in the sky
He halted on his shrivelled thigh:
His natural might had ebbed away,
Vanquished in that tremendous fray.

Not wounded he in nobler part
Nor smitten in life's fount, the heart:
But lust was shaken from his throne
And his foul empire overthrown.

Whereby we clearly learn aright
That man is whelmed by deadly night,
Unless he own God conqueror
And strive against His will no more.

Yet happier he whom rising morn
Shall find of nature's strength forlorn,
Whose warring flesh hath shrunk away,
Palsied by virtue's puissant sway.

And then at length let darkness flee,
Which all too long held us in fee,
'Mid wildering shadows made us stray
And led in devious tracks our way.

We pray Thee, Rising Light serene,
E'en as Thyself our hearts make clean:
Let no deceit our lips defile

Nor let our souls be vexed by guile.

O keep us, as the hours proceed,
From lying word and evil deed,
Our roving eyes from sin set free,
Our body from impurity.

For thou dost from above survey
The converse of each fleeting day:
Thou dost foresee from morning light
Our every deed, until the night.

Justice and judgment dwell with Thee,
Whatever is, Thine eye doth see:
Thou know'st what human hearts conceive
And none Thy wisdom may deceive.

III. HYMNUS ANTE CIBUM

O crucifer bone, lucisator,
omniparens, pie, verbigena,
edite corpore virgineo,
sed prius in genitore potens,
astra, solum, mare quam fierent: 5

Huc nitido precor intuitu
flecte salutiferam faciem,
fronte serenus et inradia,
nominis ut sub honore tui
has epulas liceat capere.   10

Te sine dulce nihil, Domine,
nec iuvat ore quid adpetere,
pocula ni prius atque cibos,
Christe, tuus favor inbuerit
omnia sanctificante fide.   15

Fercula nostra Deum sapiant,
Christus et influat in pateras:
seria, ludicra, verba, iocos,
denique quod sumus aut agimus,
trina superne regat pietas.   20

Hic mihi nulla rosae spolia,
nullus aromate fragrat odor,
sed liquor influit ambrosius
nectareamque fidem redolet
fusus ab usque Patris gremio.   25

Sperne camena leves hederas,
cingere tempora quis solita es,
sertaque mystica dactylico
texere docta liga strophio,
laude Dei redimita comas.   30

Quod generosa potest anima,
lucis et aetheris indigena,
solvere dignius obsequium,
quam data munera si recinat
artificem modulata suum?   35

Ipse homini quia cuncta dedit,
quae capimus dominante manu,
quae polus aut humus aut pelagus
aere, gurgite, rure creant,
haec mihi subdidit et sibi me.   40

Callidus inlaqueat volucres
aut pedicis dolus aut maculis,
inlita glutine corticeo
vimina plumigeram seriem
inpediunt et abire vetant.   45

Ecce per aequora fluctivagos
texta greges sinuosa trahunt:
piscis item sequitur calamum

raptus acumine vulnifico
credula saucius ora cibo.   50

  Fundit opes ager ingenuas
dives aristiferae segetis:
his ubi vitea pampineo
brachia palmite luxuriant,
pacis alumna ubi baca viret.   55

  Haec opulentia Christicolis
servit et omnia suppeditat:
absit enim procul ilia fames,
caedibus ut pecudum libeat
sanguineas lacerare dapes.   60

  Sint fera gentibus indomitis
prandia de nece quadrupedum:
nos oleris coma, nos siliqua
feta legumine multimodo
paverit innocuis epulis.   65

  Spumea mulctra gerunt niveos
ubere de gemino latices,
perque coagula densa liquor
in solidum coit et fragili
lac tenerum premitur calatho.   70

  Mella recens mihi Cecropia
nectare sudat olente favus:
haec opifex apis aerio
rore liquat tenuique thymo,
nexilis inscia connubii.   75

Hinc quoque pomiferi nemoris
munera mitia proveniunt,
arbor onus tremefacta suum
deciduo gravis imbre pluit
puniceosque iacit cumulos.　　　80

Quae veterum tuba, quaeve lyra
flatibus inclita vel fidibus
divitis omnipotentis opus,
quaeque fruenda patent homini
laudibus aequiparare queat?　　　85

Te Pater optime mane novo,
solis et orbita cum media est,
te quoque luce sub occidua
sumere cum monet hora cibum,
nostra Deus canet harmonia.　　　90

Quod calet halitus interior,
corde quod abdita vena tremit,
pulsat et incita quod resonam
lingua sub ore latens caveam,
laus superi Patris esto mihi.　　　95

Nos igitur tua sancte manus
caespite conposuit madido
effigiem meditata suam,
utque foret rata materies
flavit et indidit ore animam.　　　100

Tunc per amoena vireta iubet
frondicomis habitare locis,
ver ubi perpetuum redolet

prataque multicolora latex
quadrifluo celer amne rigat.   105

  Haec tibi nunc famulentur, ait,
usibus omnia dedo tuis:
sed tamen aspera mortifero
stipite carpere poma veto,
qui medio viret in nemore.   110

  Hic draco perfidus indocile
virginis inlicit ingenium,
ut socium malesuada virum
mandere cogeret ex vetitis
ipsa pari peritura modo.   115

  Corpora mutua--nosse nefas--
post epulas inoperta vident,
lubricus error et erubuit:
tegmina suta parant foliis,
dedecus ut pudor occuleret.   120

  Conscia culpa Deum pavitans
sede pia procul exigitur.
innuba fernina quae fuerat,
coniugis excipit inperium,
foedera tristia iussa pati.   125

  Auctor et ipse doli coluber
plectitur inprobus, ut mulier
colla trilinguia calce terat:
sic coluber muliebre solum
suspicit atque virum mulier.   130

His ducibus vitiosa dehinc
posteritas ruit in facinus,
dumque rudes imitatur avos,
fasque nefasque simul glomerans
inpia crimina morte luit.　　　135

　Ecce venit nova progenies,
aethere proditus alter homo,
non luteus, velut ille prior:
sed Deus ipse gerens hominem,
corporeisque carens vitiis.　　　140

　Fit caro vivida sermo Patris,
numine quam rutilante gravis
non thalamo, neque iure tori,
nec genialibus inlecebris
intemerata puella parit.　　　145

　Hoc odium vetus illud erat,
hoc erat aspidis atque hominis
digladiabile discidium,
quod modo cernua femineis
vipera proteritur pedibus.　　　150

　Edere namque Deum merita
omnia virgo venena domat:
tractibus anguis inexplicitis
virus inerme piger revomit,
gramine concolor in viridi.　　　155

　Quae feritas modo non trepidat,
territa de grege candidulo?
inpavidas lupus inter oves

tristis obambulat et rabidum
sanguinis inmemor os cohibet.   160

  Agnus enim vice mirifica
ecce leonibus inperitat:
exagitansque truces aquilas
per vaga nubila, perque notos
sidere lapsa columba fugat.   165

  Tu mihi Christe columba potens,
sanguine pasta cui cedit avis,
tu niveus per ovile tuum
agnus hiare lupum prohibes,
sub iuga tigridis ora premens.   170

  Da locuples Deus hoc famulis
rite precantibus, ut tenui
membra cibo recreata levent,
neu piger inmodicis dapibus
viscera tenta gravet stomachus.   175

  Haustus amarus abesto procul,
ne libeat tetigisse manu
exitiale quid aut vetitum:
gustus et ipse modum teneat,
sospitet ut iecur incolume.   180

  Sit satis anguibus horrificis,
liba quod inpia corporibus
ah miseram peperere necem,
sufficiat semel ob facinus
plasma Dei potuisse mori.   185

Oris opus, vigor igneolus
non moritur, quia flante Deo
conpositus superoque fluens
de solio Patris artificis
vim liquidae rationis habet.   190

Viscera mortua quin etiam
post obitum reparare datur,
eque suis iterum tumulis
prisca renascitur effigies
pulvereo coeunte situ.   195

Credo equidem, neque vana fides,
corpora vivere more animae:
nam modo corporeum memini
de Phlegethonte gradu facili
ad superos remeasse Deum.   200

Spes eadem mea membra manet,
quae redolentia funereo
iussa quiescere sarcophago
dux parili redivivus humo
ignea Christus ad astra vocat.   205

III. HYMN BEFORE MEAT

Blest Cross-bearer, Source of good,
  Light-creating, Word-begot,
Gracious child of maidenhood,
  Bosomed in the Fatherhood,
When earth, sea and stars were not.

With Thy cloudless, healing gaze
  Shine upon me from above:
Let Thine all-enlightening rays
  Bless this meal and quicken praise,
Praise unto Thy name of Love.

Lord, without Thee nought is sweet,
  Nought my life can satisfy,
If Thy favour make not meet
  What I drink and what I eat;
Let faith all things sanctify!

O'er this bread God's grace be poured,
  Christ's sweet fragrance fill the bowl!
Rule my converse, Triune Lord,
  Sober thought and sportive word,
All my acts and all my soul.

Spoils of rose-trees are not spent,
  Nor rich unguents on my board:
But ambrosial sweets are sent,
  Of faith's nectar redolent,
From the bosom of my Lord.

Scorn, my Muse, light ivy-leaves
  Wherewith custom wreathed thy brow:
Love a mystic crown conceives
  And a rhythmic garland weaves:
Bind on thee God's praises now.

What more worthy gift can I,
  Child of light and aether, bring
Than for boons the Maker high
  From His bounty doth supply
Lovingly my thanks to sing?

He hath set 'neath our command
  All that ever rose to be,
All that sky and sea and land
  Breed in air, in glebe and sand,
Made my slaves, His own made me.

Fowler's craft with gin and net
  Feathered tribes of heaven ensnares:
Osier twigs with lime o'erset
  That their airy flight may let
His relentless guile prepares.

Lo! with woven mesh the seine
  Swimming shoals draws from the wave:
Nor do fish the bait disdain

Till they feel the barb's swift pain,
Captives of the food they crave.

Native wealth that knows no fail,
  Golden wheat springs from the field:
Tendrils lush o'er vineyards trail,
  Nursed of Peace the olives pale
Berries green unbidden yield.

Christ's grace fills His people's need
  With these mercies ever fresh:
Far from us be that foul greed,
  Gluttony that loves to feed
On slain oxen's bloodstained flesh.

Leave to the barbarian brood
  Banquet of the slaughtered beast:
Ours the homely, garden food,
  Greenstuff manifold and good
And the lentils' harmless feast.

Foaming milkpails bubble o'er
  With the udders' snowy stream,
Which in thickening churns we pour
  Or in wicker baskets store,
As the cheese is pressed from cream.

Honey's nectar for our use
  From the new-made comb is shed:
Which the skilful bee imbues
  With thyme's scent and airy dews,
Plying lonely toils unwed.

Orchard-groves now mellowed o'er
  Bounteously their fruitage shed:
See! like rain on forest floor
  Shaken trees their riches pour,
High-heaped apples, ripe and red.

What great trumpet voice or lyre
  Famed of yore could fitly praise
Gifts of the Almighty Sire,
  Blessings that His own require,
Richly lavished through their days?

When morn breaks upon our sight,
  Hymns, O Lord, to Thee shall ring:
Thee, when streams the midday light,
  Thee, when shadows of the night
Bid us sup, our voices sing.

For my body's vital heat,
  For my heart-blood's pulsing vein,
For my tongue and speech complete
  Unto Thee, Most High, 'tis meet
That I raise my grateful strain.

'Twas, O Holy One, Thy care
  Wrought us from the plastic clay,
Made us Thine own image bear,
  And for our perfection fair
Did Thy Breath to man convey.

On the twain Thou didst bestow
  Leafy bowers in pleasaunce fair:
Where spring's scents for aye did blow,

And four stately streams did flow
O'er meads pied with blossoms rare.

"All this realm ye now shall sway:"
  (Saidst Thou) "use it at your will,
Yet 'tis death your hands to lay
  On the Tree, whose verdant sway
Doth the midmost garden fill."

Then the Serpent's guileful hate
  Would not innocency spare:
Bade the maiden urge her mate
  With the fruit his lips to sate,
Nor 'scaped she the self-same snare.

Each their nakedness perceives
  When the feast they once partook:
Smit with shame their conscience grieves:
  Wove they coverings of leaves
Shielding from lascivious look.

Far they both in terror fled
  Thrust from dwelling of the pure:
She who erst had dwelt unwed
  Subject to her spouse was led,
Bidden Hymen's bonds endure.

On the Serpent, too, His seal
  God hath set, Who guile abhorred,
Doomed in triple neck to feel
  Impress of the woman's heel,
Fearing her, who feared her lord.

Thus sin in our parents sown
  Brought forth ruin for the race;
Good and evil having grown
  From that primal root alone,
Nought but death could guilt efface.

But the Second Man behold
  Come to re-create our kin:
Not formed after common mould
  But our God (O Love untold!)
Made in flesh that knows not sin.

Word of God incarnated,
  By His awful power conceived,
Whom a maiden yet unwed,
  Innocent of marriage-bed,
In her virgin womb received.

Now we see the Serpent lewd
  'Neath the woman's heel downtrod:
Whence there sprang the deadly feud,
  Strife for ages unsubdued,
'Twixt mankind and foe of God.

Yet God's mother, Maid adored,
  Robbed sin's poison of its bane,
And the Snake, his green coils lowered,
  Writhing on the sod, outpoured
Harmless now his venom's stain.

What fierce brute that doth not flee
  Lambs of Christ, white-robed and clean?
'Midst the flock from fear set free,

Slinks the drear wolf sullenly,
Checked his maw and tamed his mien.

Wondrous change! restrained by love
   Lions the mild lamb obey:
Eagles wild, before the dove
   Fluttering from the stars above,
Speed o'er cloudy winds away.

Thou, O Christ, my Dove dost reign
   Where the vulture gnaws no more:
Thou dost, snow-white Lamb, enchain
   Tigers fierce, and wolves restrain
Gaping at the sheepfold's door.

God of Love, Thy servants we
   Pray Thee now to grant our prayer
That our feast may frugal be,
   Nor that we dishonour Thee
By coarse surfeit of rich fare.

May we taste no bitter gall
   In our cup, nor handle we
Aught of death or harm at all,
   Nor intemperately fall
Into gross debauchery.

Be the powers of Hell content
   With their primal fraud, whereby
Death into this world was sent,
   And that, for sin's chastisement,
God's own creatures once should die.

But in us God's Breath of fire
  Cannot lose its vital force:
Never can its might expire,
  Flowing from the Eternal Sire,
Who of Reason's strength is source.

Nay, from out death's chilling tomb
  Mortal atoms shall arise:
Man from earth's vast, hidden womb
  Other, yet the same, shall bloom,
Dust re-made in glorious guise.

'Tis my faith--and faith not vain--
  Bodies live e'en as the soul:
Since I hold in memory plain
  God as man uprose again,
Loosed from Hell, to His true goal.

Whence from Him the hope I reap
  That these limbs the same shall rise,
Which enwrapped in balmy sleep
  Christ the Risen safe shall keep
Till He call me to the skies.

IV. HYMNUS POST CIBUM

Pastis visceribus ciboque sumpto,
quem lex corporis inbecilla poscit,
laudem lingua Deo patri rependat;
  Patri, qui Cherubin sedile sacrum,
nec non et Seraphin suum supremo   5
subnixus solio tenet regitque.

  Hic est, quem Sabaoth Deum vocamus,
expers principii carensque fine,
rerum conditor et repertor orbis:
  fons vitae liquida fluens ab arce,   10
infusor fidei, sator pudoris,
mortis perdomitor, salutis auctor.

  Omnes quod sumus aut vigemus, inde est:
regnat Spiritus ille sempiternus
a Christo simul et Parente missus.   15
  Intrat pectora candidus pudica,
quae templi vice consecrata rident,
postquam conbiberint Deum medullis.

  Sed si quid vitii dolive nasci
inter viscera iam dicata sensit,   20
ceu spurcum refugit celer sacellum.

Taetrum flagrat enim vapore crasso
horror conscius aestuante culpa
offensumque bonum niger repellit.

   Nec solus pudor innocensve votum   25
templum constituunt perenne Christo
in cordis medii sum ac recessu:
  sed ne crapula ferveat cavendum est,
quae sedem fidei cibis refertam
usque ad congeriem coartet intus.   30

   Parcis victibus expedita corda
infusum melius Deum receptant.
Hic pastus animae est, saporque verus:
  sed nos tu gemino fovens paratu
artus atque animas utroque pastu   35
confirmas Pater ac vigore conples.

   Sic olim tua praecluens potestas
inter raucisonos situm leones,
inlapsis dapibus virum refovit.
  Illum fusile numen execrantem   40
et curvare caput sub expolita
aeris materia nefas putantem

   Plebs dirae Babylonis ac tyrannus
morti subdiderant, feris dicarant
saevis protinus haustibus vorandum.   45
  O semper pietas fidesque tuta!
lambunt indomiti virum leones
intactumque Dei tremunt alumnum.

Adstant cominus et iubas reponunt,
mansuescit rabies fameque blanda   50
praedam rictibus ambit incruentis.
  Sed cum tenderet ad superna palmas
expertumque sibi Deum rogaret,
clausus iugiter indigensque victu:

  Iussus nuntius advolare terris,   55
qui pastum famulo daret probato,
raptim desilit obsequente mundo.
  Cernit forte procul dapes inemptas,
quas messoribus Abbacuc propheta
agresti bonus exhibebat arte.   60

  Huius caesarie manu prehensa
plenis, sicut erat, gravem canistris
suspensum rapit et vehit per auras.
  Tum raptus simul ipse prandiumque
sensim labitur in lacum leonum,   65
et, quas tunc epulas gerebat, offert:

  Sumas laetus, ait, libensque carpas,
quae summus Pater, angelusque Christi
mittunt liba tibi sub hoc periclo.
  His sumptis Danielus excitavit   70
in caelum faciem ciboque fortis
Amen reddidit, Halleluia dixit.

  Sic nos muneribus tuis refecti,
largitor Deus omnium bonorum,
grates reddimus et sacramus hymnos.   75
  Tu nos tristifico velut tyranno
mundi scilicet inpotentis actu

conclusos regis et feram repellis,

  Quae circumfremit ac vorare temptat
insanos acuens furore dentes,   80
cur te, summe Deus, precemur unum.
  Vexamur, premimur, malis rotamur;
oderunt, lacerant, trahunt, lacessunt,
iuncta est suppliciis fides iniquis.

  Nec defit tamen anxiis medela;   85
nam languente trucis leonis ira
inlapsae superingeruntur escae.
  Quas si quis sitienter hauriendo
non gustu tenui, sed ore pleno
internis velit inplicare venis,   90

  Hic sancto satiatus ex propheta,
iustorum capiet cibos virorum,
qui fructum domino metunt perenni.
  Nil est dulcius ac magis saporum,
nil quod plus hominem iuvare possit,   95
quam vatis pia praecinentis orsa.

  His sumptis licet insolens potestas
pravum iudicet, inrogetque mortem,
inpasti licet inruant leones,
  nos semper Dominum patrem fatentes   100
in te, Christe Deus, loquemur unum
constanterque tuam crucem feremus.

IV. HYMN AFTER MEAT

Refreshed we rise, and for this bread that feeds,
By law of man's weak flesh, our daily needs,
  Let every tongue, the Father's praises sing;
The Father Who on His exalted throne,
O'er Cherubim and Seraphim, alone
  Reigns in His majesty, Eternal King.

God of Sabaoth is His name: 'tis He
Who ne'er began and ne'er shall cease to be,
  Builder of worlds created at His word;
Fountain of Life that flows from out the sky,
He breathes within us Faith and Purity,
  Great Conqueror of Death, Salvation's Lord.

From Him each creature life and vigour gains,
And over all the Eternal Spirit reigns
  Who cometh from the Father and the Son:
When, dovelike, on pure hearts the heavenly Guest
Descends, they are by God's own presence blest,
  As temples where His holy work is done.

But if the taint of vice or guile arise
Within the consecrated shrine, He flies
  With speed from out the sin-defiled cell;

For, driven forth by guilt's black, surging tide,
The offended Godhead may not there abide
  Where conscious sin and noisome foulness dwell.

Not chastity nor childlike faith alone
Build up for Christ an everlasting throne
  Deep in the inmost heart, devoid of shame:
But watchful ever must His servants be,
Lest the dark power of sated gluttony
  Should bind about the abode of faith its chain.

Yet simple saints, content with frugal fare,
More surely find the Spirit present there,
  Who is our soul's true strength and heavenly food:
Thy love for us a twofold feast supplies,
O Father, whence the soul may strengthened rise
  And eke the body gain new hardihood.

Thus, fed and sheltered by Thy matchless might,
The lions' hideous roar could not affright
  Thy loyal servant in the days of old:
He boldly cursed the molten deity
And stood with stubborn head uplifted high
  That scorned to bow before a god of gold.

Then Babylon's vile mob with fury glows;
Death is his doom; and straight the tyrant throws
  The youth to be his savage lions' prey:
But faith and piety Thou still dost save,
For lo! the untamed brutes no longer rave,
  But round God's unscathed child they gently play.

Close by his side they stand with drooping mane,
The grisly, gaping jaws from blood refrain
  And with rough tongues their whilom prey caress:
But when in prayer he raised his hands to heaven
And called the God, from Whom such help was given,
  Close-prisoned, hungry, and in sore distress,

A winged messenger to earth He sends,
Who swiftly through the parting clouds descends
  To feed His servant, proven by the test:
By chance he sees from far the unbought fare
Which the good seer Habakkuk's kindly care
  With rustic art had for the reapers dressed:

Then, grasping in strong hand the prophet's hair,
He bears him gently through the rushing air,
  Still burdened with the platter's savoury load,
Till o'er the lions' den at last they stayed
And straightway to the starving youth displayed
  The food thus brought, by God's good grace bestowed.

"Take this with joy," he said, "and thankful feed,
The bread that in thy hour of direst need,
  By the great Father sent, Christ's angel brings."
Then Daniel lifts his eyes to heaven above
And, strengthened by the wondrous gift of love,
  "Amen!" he cries, and Alleluia sings.

Thus, therefore, by Thy bounties now restored,
Giver of all things good, Almighty Lord,
  We render thanks and sing glad hymns to Thee:
Though prisoned in an evil world we dwell
Where sin's grim tyrant rules, Thou dost repel

With sovran power our mortal enemy.

He roars around us, and would fain devour,
Grinding his angry teeth when 'gainst his power
  In Thee alone, O God, we still confide:
By evil things we are beset and vexed,
Tormented, hated, harassed and perplexed,
  Our faith by cruel suffering sorely tried,

Yet help ne'er fails us in our time of need,
For Thou canst quell the lions' rage, and feed
  Our hungry spirits with celestial fare:
And if some soul no meagre taste would gain
Of that repast, but thirstily is fain
  Full measure of the heavenly sweets to share,

He by the holy seers of old is fed,
And shall partake the loyal reapers' bread
  Who labour in the eternal Master's field:
For nothing sweeter than the Word can be
That fell from righteous lips, once touched by Thee,
  And nought can richer grace to mortals yield.

With this sustained, though vaunting tyranny
By unjust judgment doom us straight to die,
  And starved lions rush these limbs to tear;
Confessing ever Thine Eternal Son,
With Thee, Almighty Father, ever one,
  His cross with faith unshaken will we bear.

V. HYMNUS AD INCENSUM LUCERNAE

Inventor rutili, dux bone, luminis,
qui certis vicibus tempora dividis,
merso sole chaos ingruit horridum,
lucem redde tuis Christe fidelibus.

Quamvis innumero sidere regiam   5
lunarique polum lampade pinxeris,
incussu silicis lumina nos tamen
monstras saxigeno semine quaerere:

Ne nesciret homo spem sibi luminis
in Christi solido corpore conditam,   10
qui dici stabilem se voluit petram,
nostris igniculis unde genus venit.

Pinguis quos olei rore madentibus
lychnis aut facibus pascimus aridis:
quin et fila favis scirpea floreis   15
presso melle prius conlita fingimus.

Vivax flamma viget, seu cava testula
sucum linteolo suggerit ebrio,
seu pinus piceam fert alimoniam,
seu ceram teretem stuppa calens bibit.   20

Nectar de liquido vertice fervidum
guttatim lacrimis stillat olentibus,
ambustum quoniam vis facit ignea
imbrem de madido flere cacumine.

Splendent ergo tuis muneribus, Pater,   25
flammis mobilibus scilicet atria,
absentemque diem lux agit aemula,
quam nox cum lacero victa fugit peplo.

Sed quis non rapidi luminis arduam
manantemque Deo cernat originem?   30
Moyses nempe Deum spinifera in rubo
vidit conspicuo lumine flammeum.

Felix, qui meruit sentibus in sacris
caelestis solii visere principem,
iussus nexa pedum vincula solvere,   35
ne sanctum involucris pollueret locum.

Hunc ignem populus sanguinis incliti
maiorum meritis tutus et inpotens,
suetus sub dominis vivere barbaris,
iam liber sequitur longa per avia: 40

qua gressum tulerant castraque caerulae
noctis per medium concita moverant,
plebem pervigilem fulgure praevio
ducebat radius sole micantior.

Sed rex Niliaci littoris invido   45
fervens felle iubet praevalidam manum
in bellum rapidis ire cohortibus

ferratasque acies clangere classicum.

Sumunt arma viri seque minacibus
accingunt gladiis, triste canit tuba: 50
hic fidit iaculis, ille volantia
praefigit calamis spicula Gnosiis.

Densetur cuneis turba pedestribus,
currus pars et equos et volucres rotas
conscendunt celeres signaque bellica   55
praetendunt tumidis clara draconibus.

Hic iam servitii nescia pristini
gens Pelusiacis usta vaporibus
tandem purpurei gurgitis hospita
rubris littoribus fessa resederat.   60

Hostis dirus adest cum duce perfido,
infert et validis praelia viribus:
Moyses porro suos in mare praecipit
constans intrepidis tendere gressibus:

praebent rupta locum stagna viantibus   65
riparum in faciem pervia, sistitur
circumstans vitreis unda liquoribus,
dum plebs sub bifido permeat aequore.

Pubes quin etiam decolor asperis
inritata odiis rege sub inpio   70
Hebraeum sitiens fundere sanguinem
audet se pelago credere concavo:

ibant praecipiti turbine percita
fluctus per medios agmina regia,
sed confusa dehinc unda revolvitur   75
in semet revolans gurgite confluo.

   Currus tunc et equos telaque naufraga
ipsos et proceres et vaga corpora
nigrorum videas nare satellitum,
arcis iustitium triste tyrannicae.   80

   Quae tandem poterit lingua retexere
laudes Christe tuas? qui domitam Pharon
plagis multimodis cedere praesuli
cogis iustitiae vindice dextera.

   Qui pontum rapidis aestibus invium   85
persultare vetas, ut refluo in salo
securus pateat te duce transitus,
et mox unda rapax devoret inpios.

   Cui ieiuna eremi saxa loquacibus
exundant scatebris, et latices novos   90
fundit scissa silex, quae sitientibus
dat potum populis axe sub igneo.

   Instar fellis aqua tristifico in lacu
fit ligni venia mel velut Atticum:
lignum est, quo sapiunt aspera dulcius;   95
uam praefixa cruci spes hominum viget.

   Inplet castra cibus tunc quoque ninguidus,
inlabens gelida grandine densius:
his mensas epulis, hac dape construunt,

quam dat sidereo Christus ab aethere.   100

Nec non imbrifero ventus anhelitu
crassa nube leves invehit alites,
quae conflata in humum, cum semel agmina
fluxerunt, reduci non revolant fuga.

Haec olim patribus praemia contulit   105
insignis pietas numinis unici,
cuius subsidio nos quoque vescimur
pascentes dapibus pectora mysticis.

Fessos ille vocat per freta seculi
discissis populum turbinibus regens   110
iactatasque animas mille laboribus
iustorum in patriam scandere praecipit.

Illic purpureis tecta rosariis
omnis fragrat humus calthaque pinguia
et molles violas et tenues crocos   115
fundit fonticulis uda fugacibus.

Illic et gracili balsama surculo
desudata fluunt, raraque cinnama
spirant et folium, fonte quod abdito
praelambens fluvius portat in exitum.   120

Felices animae prata per herbida
concentu parili suave sonantibus
hymnorum modulis dulce canunt melos,
calcant et pedibus lilia candidis.

Sunt et spiritibus saepe nocentibus   125
paenarum celebres sub Styge feriae
illa nocte, sacer qua rediit Deus
stagnis ad superos ex Acheronticis.

Non sicut tenebras de face fulgida
surgens oceano Lucifer inbuit,   130
sed terris Domini de cruce tristibus
maior sole novum restituens diem.

Marcent suppliciis tartara mitibus,
exultatque sui carceris otio
functorum populus liber ab ignibus,   135
nec fervent solito flumina sulphure.

Nos festis trahimus per pia gaudia
noctem conciliis votaque prospera
certatim vigili congerimus prece
extructoque agimus liba sacrario.   140

Pendent mobilibus lumina funibus,
quae suffixa micant per laquearia,
et de languidulis fota natatibus
lucem perspicuo flamma iacit vitro.

Credas stelligeram desuper aream   145
ornatam geminis stare trionibus,
et qua bosporeum temo regit iugum,
passim purpureos spargier hesperos.

O res digna, Pater, quam tibi roscidae
noctis principio grex tuus offerat,   150
lucem, qua tribuis nil pretiosius,

lucem, qua reliqua praemia cernimus.

Tu lux vera oculis, lux quoque sensibus,
intus tu speculum, tu speculum foris,
lumen, quod famulans offero, suscipe,   155
tinctum pacifici chrismatis unguine.

Per Christum genitum, summe Pater, tuum,
in quo visibilis stat tibi gloria,
qui noster Dominus, qui tuus unicus
spirat de patrio corde paraclitum.   160

Per quem splendor, honos, laus, sapientia,
maiestas, bonitas, et pietas tua
regnum continuat numine triplici
texens perpetuis secula seculis.

V. HYMN FOR THE LIGHTING OF THE LAMPS

Blest Lord, Creator of the glowing light,
  At Whose behest the hours successive move,
  The sun has set: black darkness broods above:
Christ! light Thy faithful through the coming night.

Thy courts are lit with stars unnumbered,
  And in the cloudless vault the pale moon rides;
  Yet Thou dost bid us seek the fire that hides
Till swift we strike it from its flinty bed.

So man may learn that in Christ's body came
  The hidden hope of light to mortals given:
  He is the Rock--'tis His own word--that riven
Sends forth to all our race the eternal flame.

From lamps that brim with rich and fragrant oil,
  Or torches dry this heaven-sent fire we feed;
  Or make us rushlights from the flowering reed
And wax, whereon the bees have spent their toil.

Bright glows the light, whether the resin thick
  Of pine-brand flares, or waxen tapers burn
  With melting radiance, or the hollow urn
Yields its stored sweetness to the thirsty wick.

Beneath the might of fire, in slow decay
  The scented tears of glowing nectar fall;
  Lower and lower droops the candle tall
And ever dwindling weeps itself away.

So by Thy gifts, great Father, hearth and hall
  Are all ablaze with points of twinkling light
  That vie with daylight spent; and vanquished Night
Rends, as she flies away, her sable pall.

Who knoweth not that from high Heaven first came
  Our light, from God Himself the rushing fire?
  For Moses erst, amid the prickly brier,
Saw God made manifest in lambent flame.

Ah, happy he! deemed worthy face to face
  To see heaven's Lord within that sacred brake;
  Bidden the sandals from his feet to take,
Nor with his shoon defile that holy place.

The mighty children of the chosen name,
  Saved by the merits of their sires, and free
  After long years of savage tyranny,
Through the drear desert followed still that flame.

Striking their camp beneath the silent night
  Where'er they went, to lead their darkling way,
  The cloud of glory lent its guiding ray
And shone more splendid than the noonday light.

But, mad with jealous fury, Egypt's king
  Calls his great host to battle for their lord:
  Swiftly the cohorts gather at his word,

And down the mail-clad lines the clarions ring.

Girding their trusty swords the warriors go
  To fill the ranks; hoarse bugles rend the air;
  These seize their massy javelins, these prepare
The death-winged arrow and the Cretan bow.

The footmen throng in close battalions pressed;
  The chariots thunder; to the saddle spring
  The riders of the Nile, as forth they fling
Egypt's proud banner with the serpent crest.

And now, forgetful of the bondage past,
  Thy children, tortured by the desert heat,
  Drag to the Red Sea's brink their weary feet,
And on its sandy margin rest at last.

See! with their forsworn king the savage foe
  Draws nigh: the threatening squadrons nearer ride;
  But ever onward urged the intrepid guide
And through the waves bade Israel fearless go.

Before that steadfast march the billows fall,
  Then raise on either hand their crystal mass,
  While through the sundered deep Thy people pass
And ocean guards them with a liquid wall.

But, mad with baffled rage, the dusky horde
  Of Egypt, by their impious despot led,
  Athirst the hated Hebrews' blood to shed
Pursued, all reckless of the o'er-arching flood.

Swift as the wind the royal squadrons ride,
  But swifter yet the crystal barriers break,
  The waves exultantly their bounds forsake
And roll together in a roaring tide.

'Mid steeds and chariots and drifting mail
  The drowned lords of Egypt found a grave
  With all their swart retainers 'neath the wave;
And in their haughty courts the mourners wail.

What tongue, O Christ, Thy glories can unfold?
  Thine was the arm, outstretched in wrath, that made
  The stricken land of Pharaoh, sore afraid,
Bow down before Thy minister of old.

Thy pathless deep did at the voice restrain
  Its surging billows, till with Thee for guide
  Thy host passed scathless, and the refluent tide
Swept down the wicked to the engulfing main.

At Thy command the desert, parched and dry,
  Breaks into laughing rills, and water clear
  Wells from the smitten rock Thy flock to cheer
And quench their thirst beneath that brazen sky.

Then Marah's bitterness grew passing sweet,
  Touched by the mystic tree; so by the grace
  Of Thine own Tree, O Christ, our sinful race
Regains its lost hopes at Thy pierced feet.

Faster than icy hail the manna falls,
  Like snow down drifting from a wintry sky;
  The feast is set: they heap the tables high

With that rich food from Thy celestial halls.

Fresh blow the breezes from the distant shore
  And bear a fluttering cloud that hides the light,
  Till the frail pinions, faltering in their flight,
Sink in the wilderness to rise no more.

How great the love of God's own Son, that shed
  Such wondrous bounty on His chosen race!
  And still to us He proffers in His grace
The mystic Feast, wherewith our souls are fed.

Through the world's raging sea He bids us come,
  And 'twixt the sundered billows guides our path,
  Till, spent and wearied with the ocean's wrath,
He calls His storm-tossed saints to Heaven and home.

There in His paradise red roses blow,
  With golden daffodils and lilies pale
  And gentle violets, and down the vale
The murmuring rivulets for ever flow.

Sweet balsams, welling from the slender tree,
  And precious spices fill the fragrant air,
  And, hiding by the stream, that blossom rare
Whose leaves the river hurries to the sea.

There the blest souls with one accord unite
  To hymn in dulcet song their Saviour's praise,
  And as the chanting quire their voices raise
They tread with shining feet the lilies bright.

Yea, e'en the spirits of the lost, that dwell
  Where the black stream of sullen Acheron flows,
  Rest on that holy night when Christ arose,
And for a while 'tis holiday in Hell.

No sun from ocean rising drives away
  Their darkness, with his flaming shafts far-hurled,
  But from the cross of Christ o'er that wan world
There streams the radiance of a new-born day.

The sulphurous floods with lessened fury glow,
  The aching limbs find respite from their pain,
  While, in glad freedom from the galling chain,
The tortured ghosts a short-lived solace know.

In holy gladness let this night be sped,
  As here we gather, Lord, to watch and pray;
  To Thee with one consent our vows we pay
And on Thy altar set the sacred Bread.

From pendent chains the lamps of crystal blaze;
  By fragrant oil sustained the clear flame glows
  With strength undimmed, and through the darkness throws
High o'er the fretted roof a golden haze,

As 'twere Heaven's starry floor our wondering eye
  Beheld, wherein the Bears their light display,
  Where Phosphor heralds the approach of day
And Hesper's radiance floods the evening sky.

Meet is the gift we offer here to Thee,
  Father of all, as falls the dewy night;
  Thine own most precious gift we bring--the light

Whereby mankind Thy other bounties see.

Thou art the Light indeed; on our dull eyes
  And on our inmost souls Thy rays are poured;
  To Thee we light our lamps: receive them, Lord,
Filled with the oil of peace and sacrifice.

O hear us, Father, through Thine only Son,
  Our Lord and Saviour, by Whose love bequeathed
  The Paraclete upon our hearts has breathed,
With Him and Thee through endless ages one.

Through Christ Thy Kingdom shall for ever be,
  Thy grace, might, wisdom, glory ever shine,
  As in the Triune majesty benign
He reigns for all eternity with Thee.

VI. HYMNUS ANTE SOMNUM

Ades Pater supreme,
quem nemo vidit unquam,
Patrisque sermo Christe,
et Spiritus benigne.

O Trinitatis huius   5
vis una, lumen unum,
Deus ex Deo perennis,
Deus ex utroque missus.

Fluxit labor diei,
redit et quietis hora,   10
blandus sopor vicissim
fessos relaxat artus.

Mens aestuans procellis
curisque sauciata
totis bibit medullis   15
obliviale poclum.

Serpit per omne corpus
Lethaea vis, nec ullum
miseris doloris aegri
patitur manere sensum.   20

Lex haec data est caducis
Deo iubente membris,
ut temperet laborem
medicabilis voluptas.

Sed dum pererrat omnes   25
quies amica venas,
pectusque feriatum
placat rigante somno:

Liber vagat per auras
rapido vigore sensus,   30
variasque per figuras,
quae sunt operta, cernit.

Quia mens soluta curis,
cui est origo caelum,
purusque fons ab aethra   35
iners iacere nescit.

Imitata multiformes
facies sibi ipsa fingit,
per quas repente currens
tenui fruatur actu.   40

Sed sensa somniantum
dispar fatigat horror,
nunc splendor intererrat
qui dat futura nosse.

Plerumque dissipatis   45
mendax imago veris
animos pavore maestos

ambage fallit atra.

Quem rara culpa morum
non polluit frequenter,   50
nunc lux serena vibrans
res edocet latentes.

At qui coinquinatum
vitiis cor inpiavit,
lusus pavore multo   55
species videt tremendas.

Hoc patriarcha noster
sub carceris catena
geminis simul ministris
interpres adprobavit.   60

Quorum reversus unus
dat poculum tyranno,
ast alterum rapaces
fixum vorant volucres.

Ipsum deinde regem   65
perplexa somniantem
monuit famem futuram
clausis cavere acervis.

Mox praesul ac tetrarches
regnum per omne iussus   70
sociam tenere virgam
dominae resedit aulae.

O quam profunda iustis

arcana per soporem
aperit tuenda Christus,   75
quam clara! quam tacenda!

    Evangelista summi
fidissimus magistri
signata quae latebant
nebulis videt remotis: 80

    ipsum tonantis agnum
de caede purpurantem,
qui conscium futuri
librum resignat unus.

    Huius manum potentem   85
gladius perarmat anceps
et fulgurans utrimque
duplicem minatur ictum.

    Quaesitor ille solus
animaeque corporisque   90
ensisque bis timendus
prima ac secunda mors est.

    idem tamen benignus
ultor retundit iram
paucosque non piorum   95
patitur perire in aevum.

    Huic inclitus perenne
tribuit Pater tribunal,
hunc obtinere iussit
nomen supra omne nomen.   100

Hic praepotens cruenti
extinctor antichristi,
qui de furente monstro
pulchrum refert tropaeum.

Quam bestiam capacem   105
populosque devorantem,
quam sanguinis charybdem
Ioannis execratur.

Haec nempe, quae sacratum
praeferre nomen ausa est,   110
imam petit gehennam
Christo perempta vero.

Tali sopore iustus
mentem relaxat heros,
ut spiritu sagaci   115
caelum peragret omne.

Nos nil meremur horum,
quos creber inplet error,
concreta quos malarum
vitiat cupido rerum.   120

Sat est quiete dulci
fessum fovere corpus:
sat, si nihil sinistrum
vanae minentur umbrae.

Cultor Dei memento   125
te fontis et lavacri
rorem subisse sanctum,

te chrismate innotatum.

Fac, cum vocante somno
castum petis cubile,   130
frontem locumque cordis
crucis figura signet.

Crux pellit omne crimen,
fugiunt crucem tenebrae:
tali dicata signo   135
mens fluctuare nescit.

Procul, o procul vagantum
portenta somniorum,
procul esto pervicaci
praestigiator astu!   140

O tortuose serpens,
qui mille per Maeandros
fraudesque flexuosas
agitas quieta corda,

Discede, Christus hic est,   145
hic Christus est, liquesce:
signum quod ipse nosti
damnat tuam catervam.

Corpus licet fatiscens
iaceat recline paullum,   150
Christum tamen sub ipso
meditabimur sopore.

VI. HYMN BEFORE SLEEP

Draw near, Almighty Father,
  Ne'er seen by mortal eye;
Come, O Thou Word eternal,
  O Spirit blest, be nigh.

One light of threefold Godhead,
  One power that all transcends;
God is of God begotten,
  And God from both descends.

The hour of rest approaches,
  The toils of day are past,
And o'er our tired bodies
  Sleep's gentle charm is cast.

The mind, by cares tormented
  Amid life's storm and stress,
Drinks deep the wondrous potion
  That brings forgetfulness.

O'er weary, toil-worn mortals
  The spells of Lethe steal;
Sad hearts lose all their sorrow,
  Nor pain nor anguish feel.

For to His frail creation
  God gave this law to keep,
That labour should be lightened
  By soft and healing sleep.

But while sweet languor wanders
  Through all the pulsing veins,
And, wrapt in dewy slumber,
  The heart at rest remains,

The soul, in wakeful vigour,
  Aloft in freedom flies,
And sees in many a semblance
  The hidden mysteries.

For, freed from care, the spirit
  That came from out the sky,
Born of the stainless aether,
  Can never idle lie.

A thousand changing phantoms
  She fashions through the night,
And 'midst a world of fancy
  Pursues her rapid flight.

But divers are the visions
  That night to dreamers shows;
Rare gleams of straying splendour
  The future may disclose;

More oft the truth is darkened,
  And lying fantasy
Deceives the affrighted sleeper

With cunning treachery.

To him whose life is holy
  The things that are concealed
Lie open to his spirit
  In radiant light revealed;

But he whose heart is blackened,
  With many a sin imbued,
Sees phantoms grim and ghastly
  That beckon and delude.

So in the Egyptian dungeon
  The patriarch of old
Unto the king's two servants
  Their fateful visions told:

And one is brought from prison
  The monarch's wine to pour,
One, on the gibbet hanging,
  Foul birds of prey devour,

He warned the king, distracted
  By riddles of the night,
To hoard the plenteous harvests
  Against the years of blight.

Soon, lord of half a kingdom,
  A mighty potentate,
He shares the royal sceptre
  And dwells in princely state.

But ah! how deep the secrets
  The holy sleeper sees
To whom Christ shows His highest,
  Most sacred mysteries.

For God's most faithful servant
  The clouds were rolled away,
And John beheld the wonders
  That sealed from mortals lay.

The Lamb of God, encrimsoned
  With sacrificial stains,
Alone the Book can open
  That destiny contains.

By His strong hand is wielded
  A keen, two-edged brand
That, flashing like the lightning,
  Smites swift on either hand.

Before His bar of judgment
  Both soul and body lie;
He whom that dread sword smiteth
  The second death shall die.

Yet mercy tempers justice,
  And few the Avenger sends
(Whose guilt is past all pardon)
  To death that never ends.

To Him the Father yieldeth
  The judgment-seat of Heaven;
To Him a Name excelling

All other names is given.

For by His strength transcendent
  Shall Antichrist be slain,
And from that raging monster
  Fair trophies shall He gain:

That all-devouring Dragon,
  With blood of martyrs red,
On whose abhorred power
  John's solemn curse is laid.

And thus the proud usurper
  Of His high name is cast
By Him, the true Christ, vanquished
  To deepest hell at last.

Upon the saint heroic
  Such wondrous slumber falls
That, in the spirit roaming,
  He treads heaven's highest halls.

We may not, in our weakness,
  To dreams like these aspire,
Whose souls are steeped in error
  And evil things desire.

Enough, if weary bodies
  In peaceful sleep may rest;
Enough, if no dark powers
  Our slumbering souls molest.

Christian! the font remember,

The sacramental vow,
The holy water sprinkled,
  The oil that marked thy brow!

When at sleep's call thou seekest
  To rest in slumber chaste,
Let first the sacred emblem
  On breast and brow be traced.

The Cross dispels all darkness,
  All sin before it flies,
And by that sign protected
  The mind all fear defies.

Avaunt! ye fleeting phantoms
  That mock our midnight hours;
Avaunt! thou great Deceiver
  With all thy guileful powers.

Thou Serpent, old and crafty,
  Who by a thousand arts
And manifold temptations
  Dost vex our sleeping hearts,

Vanish! for Christ is with us;
  Away! 'tis Christ the Lord:
The sign thou must acknowledge
  Condemns thy hellish horde.

And, though the weary body
  Relaxed in sleep may be,
Our hearts, Lord, e'en in slumber,
  Shall meditate on Thee.

VII. HYMNUS IEIUNANTIUM

O Nazarene, lux Bethlem, verbum Patris,
quem partus alvi virginalis protulit,
adesto castis Christe parsimoniis,
festumque nostrum rex serenus adspice,
ieiuniorum dum litamus victimam.   5

Nil hoc profecto purius mysterio,
quo fibra cordis expiatur uvidi,
intemperata quo domantur viscera,
arvina putrem ne resudans crapulam
obstrangulatae mentis ingenium premat.   10

Hinc subiugatur luxus et turpis gula,
vini atque somni degener socordia,
libido sordens, inverecundus lepos,
variaeque pestes languidorum sensuum
parcam subactae disciplinam sentiunt.   15

Nam si licenter diffluens potu et cibo
ieiuna rite membra non coerceas,
sequitur frequenti marcida oblectamine
scintilla mentis ut tepescat nobilis,
animusque pigris stertat in praecordiis.   20

Frenentur ergo corporum cupidines,
detersa et intus emicet prudentia:
sic excitato perspicax acumine
liberque flatu laxiore spiritus
rerum parentem rectius precabitur.   25

Elia tali crevit observantia,
vetus sacerdos, ruris hospes aridi:
fragore ab omni quem remotum et segregem
sprevisse tradunt criminum frequentiam,
casto fruentem syrtium silentio.   30

Sed mox in auras igneis iugalibus
curruque raptus evolavit praepete,
ne de propinquo sordium contagio
dirus quietum mundus adflaret virum,
olim probatis inclitum ieiuniis.   35

Non ante caeli principem septemplicis
Moyses tremendi fidus interpres throni
potuit videre, quam decem recursibus
quater volutis sol peragrans sidera
omni carentem cerneret substantia.   40

Victus precanti solus in lacrimis fuit:
nam flendo pernox inrigatum pulverem
humi madentis ore pressit cernuo,
donec loquentis voce praestrictus Dei
expavit ignem non ferendum visibus.   45

Ioannis huius artis haud minus potens,
Dei perennis praecucurrit filium,

curvos viarum qui retorsit tramites
et flexuosa conrigens dispendia
dedit sequendam calle recto lineam.   50

  Hanc obsequelam praeparabat nuntius
mox adfuturo construens iter Deo,
clivosa planis, confragosa ut lenibus
converterentur, neve quidquam devium
inlapsa terris inveniret veritas.   55

  Non usitatis ortus his natalibus
oblita lactis iam vieto in pectore
matris tetendit serus infans ubera:
nec ante partu de senili effusus est,
quam praedicaret virginem plenam Deo.   60

  Post in patentes ille solitudines
amictus hirtis bestiarum pellibus
setisve tectus hispida et lanugine
secessit, horrens inquinari et pollui
contaminatis oppidorum moribus.   65

  Illic dicata parcus abstinentia
potum cibumque vir severae industriae
in usque serum respuebat vesperum,
parvum locustis et favorum agrestium
liquore pastum corpori suetus dare.   70

  Hortator ille primus et doctor novae
fuit salutis, nam sacrato in flumine
veterum piatas lavit errorum notas:
sed tincta postquam membra defaecaverat,
caelo refulgens influebat spiritus.   75

Hoc ex lavacro labe dempta criminum
ibant renati non secus, quam si rudis
auri recocta vena pulchrum splendeat,
micet metalli sive lux argentei,
sudum polito praenitens purgamine.   80

Referre prisci stemma mine ieiunii
libet fideli proditum volumine,
ut diruendae civitatis incolis
fulmen benigni mansuefactum Patris
pie repressis ignibus pepercerit.   85

Gens insolenti praepotens iactantia
pollebat olim, quam fluentem nequiter
conrupta vulgo solverat lascivia,
et inde bruto contumax fastidio
cultum superni negligebat numinis.   90

Offensa tandem iugis indulgentiae
censura iustis excitatur motibus,
dextram perarmat rhompheali incendio
nimbos crepantes et fragosos turbines
vibrans tonantum nube flammarum quatit.   95

Sed paenitendi dum datur diecula,
si forte vellent inprobam libidinem
veteresque nugas condomare ac frangere,
suspendit ictum terror exorabilis
paullumque dicta substitit sententia.   100

Ionam prophetam mitis ultor excitat,
paenae inminentis iret ut praenuntius,
sed nosset ille qui minacem iudicem

servare malle, quam ferire ac plectere,
tectam latenter vertit in Tharsos fugam.   105

  Celsam paratis pontibus scandit ratem,
udo revincta fune puppis solvitur,
itur per altum, fit procellosum mare:
tum causa tanti quaeritur periculi,
sors in fugacem missa vatem decidit.   110

  Iussus perire solus e cunctis reus,
cuius voluta crimen urna expresserat,
praeceps rotatur et profundo inmergitur:
exceptus inde beluinis faucibus
alvi capacis vivus hauritur specu.   115

         *   *   *   *   *

  Intactus exin tertiae noctis vice
monstri vomentis pellitur singultibus,
qua murmuranti fine fluctus frangitur,
salsosque candens spuma tundit pumices,
ructatus exit seque servatum stupet.   130

  In Ninivitas se coactus percito
gressu reflectit, quos ut increpaverat
pudenda censor inputans opprobria;
Inpendet, inquit, ira summi vindicis,
urbemque flamma mox cremabit, credite.   135

  Apicem deinceps ardui montis petit
visurus inde conglobatum turbidae
fumum ruinae cladis et dirae struem,
tectus flagellis multinodis germinis,

nato et repente perfruens umbraculo.   140

   Sed maesta postquam civitas vulnus novi
hausit doloris, heu supremum palpitat:
cursant per ampla congregatim moenia
plebs et senatus, omnis aetas civium,
pallens iuventus, eiulantes feminae.   145

   Placet frementem publicis ieiuniis
placare Christum, mos edendi spernitur,
glaucos amictus induit monilibus
matrona demptis, proque gemma et serico
crinem fluentem sordidus spargit cinis.   150

   Squalent recincta veste bullati patres,
setasque plangens turba sumit textiles,
inpexa villis virgo bestialibus
nigrante vultum contegit velamine,
iacens arenis et puer provolvitur.   155

   Rex ipse Coos aestuantem murices
laenam revulsa dissipabat fibula,
gemmas virentes et lapillos sutiles,
insigne frontis exuebat vinculum
turpi capillos inpeditus pulvere.   160

   Nullus bibendi, nemo vescendi memor,
ieiuna mensas pubis omnis liquerat,
quin et negato lacte vagientium
fletu madescunt parvulorum cunulae,
sucum papillae parca nutrix derogat.   165

Greges et ipsos claudit armentalium
sollers virorum cura, ne vagum pecus
contingat ore rorulenta gramina,
potum strepentis neve fontis hauriant,
vacuis querelae personant praesepibus.   170

Mollitus his et talibus brevem Deus
iram refrenat temperans oraculum
prosper sinistrum, prona nam clementia
haud difficulter supplicem mortalium
solvit reatum fitque fautrix flentium.   175

Sed cur vetustae gentis exemplum oquor?
pridem caducis cum gravatus artubus
Iesus dicato corde ieiunaverit,
praenuncupatus ore qui prophetico
Emanuel est, sive NOBISCUM DEUS.   180

Qui corpus istud molle naturaliter
captumque laxo sub voluptatum iugo
virtutis arta lege fecit liberum:
emancipator servientis plasmatis
regnantis ante victor et cupidinis.   185

Inhospitali namque secretus loco
quinis diebus octies labentibus
nullam ciborum vindicavit gratiam,
firmans salubri scilicet ieiunio
vas adpetendis inbecillum gaudiis.   190

Miratus hostis posse limum tabidum
tantum laboris sustinere ac perpeti,
explorat arte sciscitator callida,

Deusne membris sit receptus terreis,
sed increpata fraude post tergum ruit.   195

  Hoc nos sequamur quisque nunc pro viribus,
quod consecrati tu magister dogmatis
tuis dedisti Christe sectatoribus,
ut, cum vorandi vicerit libidinem,
late triumphet inperator spiritus.   200

  Hoc est, quod atri livor hostis invidet,
mundi polique quod gubernator probat,
altaris aram quod facit placabilem,
quod dormientis excitat cordis fidem,
quod limat aegram pectoris rubiginem.   205

  Perfusa non sic amne flamma extinguitur,
nec sic calente sole tabescunt nives,
ut turbidarum scabra culparum seges
vanescit almo trita sub ieiunio,
si blanda semper misceatur largitas.   210

  Est quippe et illud grande virtutis genus
operire nudos, indigentes pascere,
opem benignam ferre supplicantibus,
unam paremque sortis humanae vicem
inter potentes atque egenos ducere.   215

  Satis beatus quisque dextram porrigit,
laudis rapacem, prodigam pecuniae,
cuius sinistra dulce factum nesciat:
illum perennes protinus conplent opes,
ditatque fructus faenerantem centuplex.   220

VII. HYMN FOR THOSE WHO FAST

O Jesus, Light of Bethlehem,
  True Son of God, Incarnate Word;
Thou offspring of a Virgin's womb,
  Be present at our frugal board;
Accept our fast, our sacrifice,
  And smile upon us, gracious Lord.

For by this holiest mystery
  The inward parts are cleansed from stain,
And, taming all the unbridled lusts,
  Our sinful flesh we thus restrain,
Lest gluttony and drunkenness
  Should choke the soul and cloud the brain.

Hence appetite and luxury
  Are forced their empire to resign;
The wanton sport, the jest obscene,
  The ignoble sway of sleep and wine,
And all the plagues of languid sense
  Feel the strict bonds of discipline.

For if, full fed with meat and drink,
  The flesh thou ne'er dost mortify,
The mind, that spark of sacred flame,

By pleasure dulled, must fail and die,
And pent in its gross prison-house
  The soul in shameful torpor lie.

So be thy carnal lusts controlled,
  So be thy judgment clear and bright;
Then shall thy spirit, swift and free,
  Be gifted with a keener sight,
And breathing in an ampler air
  To the All-Father pray aright.

Elias by such abstinence,
  Seer of the desert, grew in grace,
Who left the madding haunts of men
  And found a peaceful resting-place,
Where, far from sinful crowds, he trod
  The pure and silent wilderness.

Till by those fiery coursers drawn
  The swift car bore him through the air,
Lest earth's defiling touch should mar
  The holiness it might not share,
Or some polluting breath disturb
  The peace attained by fast and prayer.

Moses, through whom from His dread throne
  The will of God to man was told,
No food might touch till through the sky
  The sun full forty times had rolled,
Ere God before him stood revealed,
  Lord of the heavens sevenfold.

Tears were his meat, while bent in prayer
  Through the long night he bowed his head
E'en to the thirsty dust, that drank
  The drops in bitter weeping shed;
Till, at God's call, he saw the flame
  No eye may bear, and was afraid.

The Baptist, too, was strong in fast--
  Forerunner in a later day
Of God's Eternal Son--who made
  The byepaths plain, the crooked way
A road direct, wherein His feet
  Might travel on without delay.

This was the messenger's great task
  Who for God's advent zealously
Prepared the way, the rough made smooth,
  The mountain levelled to the sea;
That, when Truth came from heaven to earth,
  All fair and straight His path should be.

He was not born in common wise,
  For dry and wrinkled was the breast
Of her that bare him late in years,
  Nor found she from her labour rest,
Till she had hailed with lips inspired
  The Maid with unborn Godhead blest.

For him the hairy skins of beasts
  Furnished a raiment rude and wild,
As forth into the lonely waste
  He fared, an unbefriended child,
Who dwelt apart, lest he should be

By evil city-life defiled.

There, vowed to abstinence, he grew
　To manhood, and with stern disdain
He turned from meat and drink, until
　He saw night's shadow fall again;
And locusts and the wild bees' store
　Sufficed his vigour to sustain.

The first was he to testify
　Of that new life which man might win;
In Jordan's consecrating stream
　He purged the stains of ancient sin,
And, as he made the body clean,
　The radiant Spirit entered in.

Forth from the holy tide they came
　Reborn, from guilt's pollution free,
As bright from out the cleansing fire
　Flows the rough gold, or as we see
The glittering silver, purged of dross,
　Flash into polished purity.

Now let us tell, from Holy Writ,
　Of olden fasts the fairest crown;
How God in pity stayed His hand,
　And spared a doomed and guilty town,
In clemency the flames withheld
　And laid His vengeful lightnings down.

A mighty race of ancient time
　Waxed arrogant in boastful pride;
Debauched were they, and borne along

On foul corruption's loathsome tide,
Till in their stiff-necked self-conceit
  They e'en the God of Heaven denied.

At last Eternal Mercy turns
  To righteous judgment, swift and dire;
He shakes the clouds; the mighty sword
  Flames in His hand, and in His ire
He wields the roaring hurricane
  'Mid murky gloom and flashing fire.

Yet in His clemency He grants
  To penitence a brief delay,
That they might burst the bonds of lust
  And put their vanities away;
His sentence given, He waits awhile
  And stays the hand upraised to slay.

To warn them of the wrath to come
  The Avenger in His mercy sent
Jonah the seer; but,--though he knew
  The threatening Judge would fain relent
Nor wished to strike,--towards Tarshish town
  The prophet's furtive course was bent.

As up the galley's side he climbed,
  They loosed the dripping rope, and passed
The harbour bar: then on them burst
  The sudden fury of the blast;
And when their peril's cause they sought,
  The lot was on the recreant cast.

The man whose guilt the urn declares

Alone must die, the rest to save;
Hurled headlong from the deck, he falls
  And sinks beneath the engulfing wave,
Then, seized by monstrous jaws, is plunged
  Into a vast and living grave.

*   *   *   *   *

At last the monster hurls him forth,
  As the third night had rolled away;
Before its roar the billows break
  And lash the cliffs with briny spray;
Unhurt the wondering prophet stands
  And hails the unexpected day.

Thus turned again to duty's path
  To Nineveh he swiftly came,
Their lusts rebuked and boldly preached
  God's judgment on their sin and shame;
"Believe!" he cried, "the Judge draws nigh
  Whose wrath shall wrap your streets in flame."

Thence to the lofty mount withdrew,
  Where he might watch the smoke-cloud lower
O'er blasted homes and ruined halls,
  And rest beneath the shady bower
Upspringing in swift luxury
  Of twining tendril, leaf and flower.

But when the guilty burghers heard
  The impending doom, a dull despair
Possessed their souls; proud senators,
  Poor craftsmen, throng the highways fair;

Pale youth with tottering age unites,
  And women's wailing rends the air.

A public fast they now decree,
  If they may thus Christ's anger stay:
No food they touch: each haughty dame
  Puts silken robes and gems away,
In sable garbed, and ashes casts
  Upon her tresses' disarray.

In dark and squalid vesture clad
  The Fathers go: the mourning crowd
Dons rough attire: in shaggy skins
  Enwrapped, fair maids their faces shroud
With dusky veils, and boyish heads
  E'en to the very dust are bowed.

The King tears off his jewelled brooch
  And rends the robe of Coan hue;
Bright emeralds and lustrous pearls
  Are flung aside, and ashes strew
The royal head, discrowned and bent,
  As low he kneels God's grace to sue.

None thought to drink, none thought to eat;
  All from the table turned aside,
And in their cradles wet with tears
  Starved babes in bitter anguish cried,
For e'en the foster-mother stern
  To little lips the breast denied.

The very flocks are closely penned
  By careful hands, lest they should gain

Sweet water from the babbling stream
  Or wandering crop the dewy plain;
And bleating sheep and lowing kine
  Within their barren stalls complain.

Moved by such penitence, full soon
  God's grace repealed the stern decree
And curbed His righteous wrath; for aye,
  When man repents, His clemency
Is swift to pardon and to hear
  His children weeping bitterly.

Yet wherefore of that bygone race
  Should we anew the story tell?
For Christ's pure soul by fasting long
  The clogging bonds of flesh did quell;
He Whom the prophet's voice foretold
  As GOD WITH US, Emmanuel.

Man's body--frail by nature's law
  And bound by pleasure's easy chain--
He freed by virtue's strong restraint,
  And gave it liberty again:
He broke the bonds of flesh, and Lust
  Was driven from his old domain.

Deep in the inhospitable wild
  For forty days He dwelt alone
Nor tasted food, till, thus prepared,
  All human weakness overthrown
By fasting's power, His mortal frame
  Rejoiced the spirit's sway to own.

The Adversary, marvelling
  To see this creature of a day
Endure such toil, spent all his guile
  To learn if God in human clay
Had come indeed; but soon rebuked
  Behind His back fled shamed away.

Therefore let each with all his might
  Follow the way the Master taught,
The law of consecrated life
  Which Christ unto His servants brought;
Till, with the lusts of flesh subdued,
  The spirit reigns o'er act and thought.

'Tis this our jealous foe abhors,
  'Tis this the Lord of earth and sky
Approves; by this the soul is made
  Thy holy altar, God Most High:
Faith stirs within the slumbering heart
  And sin's corroding power must fly.

Swifter than water quenches fire,
  Swifter than sunshine melts the snow,
Crushed out by soul-restoring fast
  Vanish the sins that rankly grow,
If hand in hand with Abstinence
  Sweet Charity doth ever go.

This too is Virtue's noble task,
  To clothe the naked, and to feed
The destitute, with kindly care
  To visit sufferers in their need;
For king and beggar each must bear

The lot by changeless Fate decreed.

Happy the man whose good right hand
 Seeks but God's praise, and flings his gold
Broadcast, nor lets his left hand know
 The gracious deed; for wealth untold
Shall crown him through eternal years
 With usury an hundredfold.

VIII. HYMNUS POST IEIUNIUM

Christe servorum regimen tuorum,
mollibus qui nos moderans habenis
leniter frenas facilique septos
      lege coerces:

ipse cum portans onus inpeditum   5
corporis duros tuleris labores,
maior exemplis famulos remisso
      dogmate palpas.

Nona submissum rotat hora solem
partibus vixdum tribus evolutis,   10
quarta devexo superest in axe
      portio lucis.

Nos brevis voti dape vindicata
solvimus festum fruimurque mensis
adfatim plenis, quibus inbuatur   15
      prona voluptas.

Tantus aeterni favor est magistri,
doctor indulgens ita nos amico
lactat hortatu, levis obsequela ut
      mulceat artus.   20

Addit et, ne quis velit invenusto
sordidus cultu lacerare frontem,
sed decus vultus capitisque pexum
     comat honorem.

Terge ieiunans, ait, omne corpus,   25
neve subducto faciem rubore
luteus tinguat color aut notetur
     pallor in ore.

Rectius laeto tegimus pudore,
quidquid ad cultum Patris exhibemus: 30
cernit occultum Deus et latentem
     munere donat.

Ille ovem morbo residem gregique
perditam sano male dissipantem
vellus adfixis vepribus per hirtae   35
     devia silvae.

Inpiger pastor revocat lupisque
gestat exclusis humeros gravatus,
inde purgatam revehens aprico
     reddit ovili: 40

Reddit et pratis viridique campo,
vibrat inpexis ubi nulla lappis
spina, nec germen sudibus perarmat
     carduus horrens:

Sed frequens palmis nemus et reflexa   45
vernat herbarum coma, tum perennis

gurgitem vivis vitreum fluentis
    laurus obumbrat.

Hisce pro donis tibi, fide pastor,
servitus quaenam poterit rependi?   50
nulla conpensant pretium salutis
    vota precantum.

Quamlibet spreto sine more pastu
sponte confectos tenuemus artus,
teque contemptis epulis rogemus   55
    nocte dieque;

Vincitur semper minor obsequentum
cura, nec munus genitoris aequat,
frangit et cratem luteam laboris
    grandior usus.   60

Ergo ne limum fragilem solutae
deserant vires et aquosus albis
humor in venis dominetur aegrum
    corpus inervans,

Laxus ac liber modus abstinendi   65
ponitur cunctis, neque nos severus
terror inpellit, sua quemque cogit
    velle potestas.

Sufficit, quidquid facias, vocato
numinis nutu prius, inchoare,   70
sive tu mensam renuas cibumve
    sumere temptes.

Adnuit dexter Deus et secundo
prosperat vultu, velut hoc salubre
fidimus nobis fore, quod dicatas　　75
　　carpimus escas.

Sit bonum, supplex precor et medelam
conferat membris, animumque pascat
sparsus in venas cibus obsecrantum
　　christicolarum.　　　　80

VIII. HYMN AFTER FASTING

O Christ, of all Thy servants Guide,
  Mild is the yoke Thou mak'st us bear,
Leading us gently by Thy side
    With gracious care.

Thy love took up our life's hard load
  And spent in grievous toils its might:
Thy bond-slaves tread the easier road
    Led by Thy light.

Nine hours have run their course away,
  The sun sped three parts of its race:
And what remains of the short day
    Fadeth apace.

The holy fast hath reached its end;
  Our table now Thou loadest, Lord:
With all Thy gifts true gladness send
    To grace our board.

Such is our Master's gentle sway,
  So kind the teaching in His school,
That all find rest who will obey
    His easy rule.

Thou would'st not have us scorn the grace
　Of cleanliness and vesture fair:
Thou lovest not a soiled face
　　And unkempt hair.

Let him that fasts, Thou saidst, be clean,
　Nor lose health's fair and ruddy glow:
Let no wan sallowness be seen
　　Upon his brow.

'Tis better in glad modesty
　Of our good works to shun display:
God sees what 'scapes our neighbour's eye
　　And will repay.

That Shepherd keen seeks one lost sheep
　Sickly and weak, strayed from the fold,
Fleece torn with briers of thickets deep,
　　Foolishly bold.

He drives the wolves far from the track:
　And found He brings on shoulders borne
To sunlit pen the wanderer back,
　　No more forlorn:

Yea, to the meads and grassy fields
　The lamb restores, where no thorn balks,
No rough burrs tear, no thistle yields
　　Its bristling stalks:

But leaves of green herbs brightly glance
　And in the grove the palm-trees dream,
And laurels shade the eddying dance

Of crystal stream.

For all these gifts, O Shepherd dear,
　What service can I render Thee?
No grateful vows my debt shall clear
　　For love so free.

Though by self-chosen fasts severe
　Our strength of limb we waste away:
Though, spurning food, we Thee revere
　By night and day:

Yet our works never can o'ertake
　Thy love or with Thy gifts compare:
Our toils this earthen vessel break,
　　The more we dare.

Therefore lest failing powers consume
　Our fragile life and shrivelled veins
Pale 'neath the tyranny of rheum
　　And weakening pains:

Thou dost not rule perpetual Lent
　For man, nor modest fare deny:
Fearless may each unto his bent
　　His wants supply.

Enough that all our acts by prayer
　Be sanctified unto Thy will,
Whether we fast, or with due care
　　Our needs fulfil.

Then shall God bless us for our good

And lead us to our soul's true wealth;
For, if but consecrated, food
   Shall bring us health.

O Lord, grant that our feast may spread
  Marrow and strength throughout our flesh:
And may all Christly souls be fed
   With vigour fresh.

IX. HYMNUS OMNIS HORAE

Da puer plectrum, choreis ut canam fidelibus
dulce carmen et melodum, gesta Christi insignia:
hunc camena nostra solum pangat, hunc laudet lyra.

Christus est, quem rex sacerdos adfuturum protinus
infulatus concinebat voce, chorda et tympano,   5
spiritum caelo influentem per medullas hauriens.

Facta nos et iam probata pangimus miracula,
testis orbis est, nec ipsa terra, quod vidit, negat,
cominus Deum docendis proditum mortalibus.

Corde natus ex parentis, ante mundi exordium   10
alpha et O cognominatus, ipse fons et clausula
omnium, quae sunt, fuerunt quaeque post futura sunt.

Ipse iussit et creata, dixit ipse, et facta sunt
terra, caelum, fossa ponti, trina rerum machina,
quaeque in his vigent sub alto solis et lunae globo.   15

Corporis formam caduci, membra morti obnoxia
induit, ne gens periret primoplasti ex germine,
merserat quam lex profundo noxialis tartaro.

O beatus ortus ille, virgo cum puerpera
edidit nostram salutem feta sancto spiritu,   20
et puer redemptor orbis os sacratum protulit.

Psallat altitudo caeli, psallite omnes angeli,
quidquid est virtutis usquam psallat in laudem Dei:
nulla linguarum silescat, vox et omnis consonet.

Ecce quem vates vetustis concinebant seculis,   25
quem prophetarum fideles paginae spoponderant,
emicat promissus olim: cuncta conlaudent eum.

Cantharis infusa lympha fit Falernum nobile,
nuntiat vinum minister esse promptum ex hydria,
ipse rex sapore tinctis obstupescit poculis.   30

Membra morbis ulcerosa, viscerum putredines
mando, ut abluantur, inquit; fit ratum, quod iusserat,
turgidam cutem repurgant vulnerum piamina.

Tu perennibus tenebris iam sepulta lumina
inlinis limo salubri, sacri et oris nectare,   35
mox apertis hac medela lux reducta est orbibus.

Increpas ventum furentem, quod procellis tristibus
vertat aequor fundo ab imo, vexet et vagam ratem:
ille iussis obsecundat, mitis unda sternitur.

Extimum vestis sacratae furtim mulier attigit,   40
protinus salus secuta est, ora pallor deserit,
sistitur rivus, cruore qui fluebat perpeti.

Exitu dulcis iuventae raptum ephebum viderat,

orba quem mater supremis funerabat fletibus:
surge, dixit: ille surgit, matri et adstans redditur.   45

Sole iam quarto carentem, iam sepulcro absconditum
Lazarum iubet vigere reddito spiramine:
fetidum iecur reductus rursus intrat halitus.

Ambulat per stagna ponti, summa calcat fluctuum,
mobilis liquor profundi pendulam praestat viam,   50
nec fatiscit unda sanctis pressa sub vestigiis.

Suetus antro bustuali sub catenis frendere,
mentis inpos efferatis percitus furoribus
prosilit ruitque supplex, Christum adesse ut senserat.

Pulsa pestis lubricorum milleformis daemonum   55
conripit gregis suilli sordida spurcamina,
seque nigris mergit undis et pecus lymphaticum.

Quinque panibus peresis et gemellis piscibus
adfatim refecta iam sunt adcubantum milia,
fertque qualus ter quaternus ferculorum fragmina.   60

Tu cibus panisque noster, tu perennis suavitas;
nescit esurire in aevum, qui tuam sumit dapem,
nec lacunam ventris inplet, sed fovet vitalia.

Clausus aurium meatus et sonorum nescius
purgat ad praecepta Christi crassa quaeque obstacula, 65
vocibus capax fruendis ac susurris pervius.

Omnis aegritudo cedit, languor omnis pellitur,
lingua fatur, quam veterna vinxerant silentia,

gestat et suum per urbem laetus aeger lectulum.

Quin et ipsum, ne salutis inferi expertes forent,   70
tartarum benignus intrat, fracta cedit ianua,
vectibus cadit revulsis cardo indissolubilis.

Illa prompta ad inruentes, ad revertentes tenax,
obice extrorsum repulso porta reddit mortuos:
lege versa et limen atrum iam recalcandum patet.   75

Sed Deus dum luce fulva mortis antra inluminat,
dum stupentibus tenebris candidum praestat diem,
tristia squalentis aethrae pallucrunt sidera.

Sol refugit et lugubri sordidus ferrugine
igneum reliquit axem seque maerens abdidit: 80
fertur horruisse mundus noctis aeternae chaos.

Solve vocem mens sonoram, solve linguam mobilem,
dic tropaeum passionis, dic triumphalem crucem,
pange vexillum, notatis quod refulget frontibus.

O novum caede stupenda vulneris miraculum!   85
hinc cruoris fluxit unda, lympha parte ex altera:
lympha nempe dat lavacrum, tum corona ex sanguine est.

Vidit anguis inmolatam corporis sacri hostiam,
vidit et fellis perusti mox venenum perdidit,
saucius dolore multo colla fractus sibilat.   90

Quid tibi, profane serpens, profuit, rebus novis
plasma primum perculisse versipelli hortamine?
diluit culpam recepto forma mortalis Deo.

Ad brevem se mortis usum dux salutis dedidit,
mortuos olim sepultos ut redire insuesceret,   95
dissolutis pristinorum vinculis peccaminum.

Tunc patres sanctique multi conditorem praevium
iam revertentem secuti tertio demum die
carnis indumenta sumunt, eque bustis prodeunt.

Cerneres coire membra de favillis aridis,   100
frigidum venis resumptis pulverem tepescere,
ossa, nervos, ac medullas glutino cutis tegi.

Post, ut occasum resolvit vitae et hominem reddidit,
arduum tribunal victor adscendit Patris,
inclitam caelo reportans passionis gloriam.   105

Macte index mortuorum, macte rex viventium,
dexter in parentis arce qui cluis virtutibus
omnium venturus inde iustus ultor criminum.

Te senes et te iuventus, parvulorum te chorus,
turba matrum virginumque simplices puellulae,   110
voce concordes pudicis perstrepant concentibus.

Fluminum lapsus et undae, littorum crepidines,
imber, aestus, nix, pruina, silva, et aura, nox, dies,
omnibus te concelebrent seculorum seculis.

IX. HYMN FOR ALL HOURS

Let me chant in sacred numbers, as I strike each sounding string,
  Chant in sweet, melodious anthems, glorious deeds of Christ our King;
He, my Muse, shall be thy story; with His praise my lyre shall ring.

When the king in priestly raiment sang the Christ that was to be,
  Voice and lute and clashing cymbal joined in joyous harmony,
While the Spirit, heaven-descended, touched his lips to prophecy.

Sing we now the works sure proven, wrought of God in mystic wise;
  Heaven is witness; earth confesses how she saw with wondering eyes
God Himself with mortals mingling, man to teach in human guise.

Of the Father's heart begotten, ere the world from chaos rose,
  He is Alpha; from that Fountain all that is and hath been flows;
He is Omega, of all things yet to come the mystic Close.

By His word was all created; He commands and lo! 'tis done;
  Earth and sky and boundless ocean, universe of three in one,
All that sees the moon's soft radiance, all that breathes beneath the sun.

He assumed this mortal body, frail and feeble, doomed to die,
  That the race from dust created might not perish utterly,
Which the dreadful Law had sentenced in the depths of Hell to lie.

O how blest that wondrous birthday, when the Maid the curse retrieved,
  Brought to birth mankind's salvation, by the Holy Ghost conceived;
And the sacred Babe, Redeemer of the world, her arms received.

Sing, ye heights of heaven, His praises; angels and archangels, sing!
  Wheresoe'er ye be, ye faithful, let your joyous anthems ring,
Every tongue His name confessing, countless voices answering.

This is He whom seer and sibyl sang in ages long gone by;
  This is He of old revealed in the page of prophecy;
Lo! He comes, the promised Saviour; let the world His praises cry!

In the urns the clear, cold water turns to juice of noblest vine,
  And the servant, drawing from them, starts to see the generous wine,
While the host, its savour tasting, wonders at the draught divine.

To the leper worn and wasted, white with many a loathsome sore,
  "Be thou cleansed," He said; "I bid it!" swift 'tis done, His words restore;
To the priest the gift he offers, clean and healthful as of yore.

On the eyes long sealed in darkness, buried in unbroken night,
  Thou didst spread Thy lips' sweet nectar, mixed with clay: then came the sight,
As Thy gracious touch all-healing brought to those dark orbs the light.

Thou didst chide the raging tempest, when the waves with foaming crest
  Leaped about the fragile vessel, buffeted and sore distressed;
Wind and wave, their fury stilling, sank to calm at Thy behest.

Once a woman's timid fingers touched Thy garment's lowest braid,
  And the pallor left her visage, healing power the touch conveyed,
For the years of pain were ended and the flow of blood was stayed.

Thou didst see men bear to burial one struck down in youth's glad tide,
  While a widowed mother followed, wailing for her boy that died;
"Rise!" Thou saidst, and led him gently to his weeping mother's side.

Lazarus, who lay in darkness till three nights had passed away,
  At Thy voice awoke to soundness, rising to the light of day,
As the breath his frame re-entered touched already with decay.

See, He walks upon the waters, treads the billow's rolling crest;
  O'er the shifting depths of ocean firm and sure His footsteps rest,
And the wave parts not asunder where those holy feet are pressed.

And the madman, chained and tortured by dark powers, from whom all fly,
  As the tombs, that were his dwelling, echo to his savage cry,
Rushes forth and falls adoring, when he sees that Christ is nigh.

Then the legion of foul spirits, driven from their human prey,
  Seize the noisome swine, that feeding high upon the hillside stray,
And the herd, in sudden frenzy, plunges in the waters grey.

"Gather in twelve woven baskets all the fragments that remain:"
  He hath fed the weary thousands, resting o'er the grassy plain,
And His power hath stayed their hunger with five loaves and fishes twain.

Thine, O Christ, is endless sweetness; Thou art our celestial Bread:
  Nevermore he knoweth hunger, who upon Thy grace hath fed,
Grace whereby no mortal body but the soul is nourished.

They that knew not speech nor language, closed to every sound their ears,
  To the Master's call responding break the barriers of years;
Now the deaf holds joyous converse and the lightest whisper hears.

Sickness at His word departed, pain and pallid languor fled,

Many a tongue, long chained in silence, words of praise and blessing said;
And the palsied man rejoicing through the city bore his bed.

Yea, that they might know salvation who in Hades' prison were pent,
  In His mercy condescending through Hell's gloomy gates He went;
Bolt and massy hinge were shattered, adamantine portals rent.

For the door that all receiveth, but releaseth nevermore,
  Opens now and, slowly turning, doth the ghosts to light restore,
Who, the eternal laws suspended, tread again its dusky floor.

But, while God with golden glory floods the murky realms of night,
  And upon the startled shadows dawns a day serene and bright,
In the darkened vault of heaven stars forlorn refuse their light.

For the sun in garb of mourning veiled his radiant orb and passed
  From his flaming path in sorrow, hiding till mankind aghast
Deemed that o'er a world of chaos Night's eternal pall was cast.

Now, my soul, in liquid measures let the sounding numbers flow;
  Sing the trophy of His passion, sing the Cross triumphant now;
Sing the ensign of Christ's glory, marked on every faithful brow.

Ah! how wondrous was the fountain flowing from His pierced side,
  Whence the blood and water mingled in a strange and sacred tide,--
Water, sign of mystic cleansing; blood, the martyr's crown of pride.

In that hour the ancient Serpent saw the holy Victim slain,
  Saw, and shed his hate envenomed, all his malice spent in vain;
See! the hissing neck is broken as he writhes in sullen pain.

Aye, what boots it, cursed Serpent, that the man God made from clay,
  Victim of thy baleful cunning, by thy lies was led astray?

God hath ta'en a mortal body and hath washed the guilt away.

Christ, our Captain, for a season deigned to dwell in Death's domain,
  That the dead, long time imprisoned, might return to life again,
Breaking by His great example ancient sins' enthralling chain.

Thus, upon the third glad morning, patriarchs and saints of yore,
  As the risen Lord ascended, followed Him who went before,
From forgotten graves proceeding, habited in flesh once more.

Limb to limb unites and rises from the ashes dry and cold,
    And the life-blood courses warmly through the frames long turned to mould,
Skin and flesh, anew created, muscle, bone and nerve enfold.

Then, mankind to life restoring, Death downtrodden 'neath His feet,
  Lo! the Victor mounts triumphant to the Father's judgment-seat,
Bringing back to heaven the glory by His passion made complete.

Hail! Thou Judge of souls departed: hail! of all the living King!
  On the Father's right hand throned, through His courts Thy praises ring,
Till at last for all offences righteous judgment Thou shalt bring.

Now let old and young uniting chant to Thee harmonious lays,
  Maid and matron hymn Thy glory, infant lips their anthem raise,
Boys and girls together singing with pure heart their song of praise.

Let the storm and summer sunshine, gliding stream and sounding shore,
  Sea and forest, frost and zephyr, day and night their Lord adore;
Let creation join to laud Thee through the ages evermore.

X. HYMNUS AD EXEQUIAS DEFUNCTI

Deus ignee fons animarum,
duo qui socians elementa
vivum simul ac moribundum
hominem Pater effigiasti:

Tua sunt, tua rector utraque,   5
tibi copula iungitur horum,
tibi, dum vegetata cohaerent,
et spiritus et caro servit.

Rescissa sed ista seorsum
solvunt hominera perimuntque,   10
humus excipit arida corpus,
animae rapit aura liquorem.

Quia cuncta creata necesse est
labefacta senescere tandem,
conpactaque dissociari,   15
et dissona texta retexi.

Hanc tu, Deus optime, mortem
famulis abolere paratus
iter inviolabile monstras,

quo perdita membra resurgant: 20

  Ut, dum generosa caducis
ceu carcere clausa ligantur,
pars illa potentior extet,
quae germen ab aethere traxit.

  Si terrea forte voluntas   25
luteum sapit et grave captat,
animus quoque pondere victus
sequitur sua membra deorsum.

  At si generis memor ignis
contagia pigra recuset,   30
vehit hospita viscera secum,
pariterque reportat ad astra.

  Nam quod requiescere corpus
vacuum sine mente videmus,
spatium breve restat, ut alti   35
repetat conlegia sensus.

  Venient cito secula, cum iam
socius calor ossa revisat
animataque sanguine vivo
habitacula pristina gestet.   40

  Quae pigra cadavera pridem
tumulis putrefacta iacebant,
volucres rapientur in auras
animas comitata priores.

  Hin

c maxima cura sepulcris   45
  inpenditur: hinc resolutos
  honor ultimus accipit artus
  et funeris ambitus ornat.

  Candore nitentia claro
  praetendere lintea mos est,   50
  adspersaque myrrha Sabaeo
  corpus medicamine servat.

  Quidnam sibi saxa cavata,
  quid pulchra volunt monumenta,
  nisi quod res creditur illis   55
  non mortua, sed data somno?

  Hoc provida Christicolarum
  pietas studet, utpote credens
  fore protinus omnia viva,
  quae nunc gelidus sopor urget.   60

  Qui iacta cadavera passim
  miserans tegit aggere terrae,
  opus exhibet ille benignum
  Christo pius omnipotenti:

  Quin lex eadem monet omnes   65
  gemitum dare sorte sub una,
  cognataque funera nobis
  aliena in morte dolere.

  Sancti sator ille Tobiae
  sacer ac venerabilis heros,   70
  dapibus iam rite paratis

ius praetulit exequiarum.

Iam stantibus ille ministris
cyathos et fercula liquit,
studioque accinctus humandi   75
fleto dedit ossa sepulcro.

Veniunt mox praemia caelo
pretiumque rependitur ingens:
nam lumina nescia solis
Deus inlita felle serenat.   80

Iam tunc docuit Pater orbis,
quam sit rationis egenis
mordax et amara medela,
cum lux animum nova vexat.

Docuit quoque non prius ullum   85
caelestia cernere regna,
quam nocte et vulnere tristi
toleraverit aspera mundi.

Mors ipsa beatior inde est,
quod per cruciamina leti   90
via panditur ardua iustis
et ad astra doloribus itur.

Sic corpora mortificata
redeunt melioribus annis,
nec post obitum recalescens   95
conpago fatiscere novit.

Haec, quae modo pallida tabo
color albidus inficit ora,
tunc flore venustior omni
sanguis cute tinget amoena.   100

Iam nulla deinde senectus
frontis decus invida carpet,
macies neque sicca lacertos
suco tenuabit adeso.

Morbus quoque pestifer, artus   105
qui nunc populatur anhelos,
sua tunc tormenta resudans
luet inter vincula mille.

Hunc eminus aere ab alto
victrix caro iamque perennis   110
cernet sine fine gementem
quos moverat ipse dolores.

Quid turba superstes inepta
clangens ululamina miscet,
cur tam bene condita iura   115
luctu dolor arguit amens?

Iam maesta quiesce querela,
lacrimas suspendite matres,
nullus sua pignora plangat,
mors haec reparatio vitae est.   120

Sic semina sicca virescunt
iam mortua iamque sepulta,
quae reddita caespite ab imo

veteres meditantur aristas.

Nunc suscipe terra fovendum,   125
gremioque hunc concipe molli:
hominis tibi membra sequestro
generosa et fragmina credo.

Animae fuit haec domus olim
factoris ab ore creatae,   130
fervens habitavit in istis
sapientia principe Christo.

Tu depositum tege corpus,
non inmemor illa requiret
sua munera fictor et auctor   135
propriique aenigmata vultus.

Veniant modo tempora iusta,
cum spem Deus inpleat omnem;
reddas patefacta necesse est,
qualem tibi trado figuram.   140

Non, si cariosa vetustas
dissolverit ossa favillis,
fueritque cinisculus arens
minimi mensura pugilli.

Nec, si vaga flamina et aurae   145
vacuum per inane volantes
tulerint cum pulvere nervos,
hominem periisse licebit.

Sed dum resolubile corpus
revocas, Deus, atque reformas,   150
quanam regione iubebis
animam requiescere puram?

Gremio senis addita sancti
recubabit, ut est Eleazar,
quem floribus undique septum   155
Dives procul adspicit ardens.

Sequimur tua dicta redemptor,
quibus atra morte triumphans
tua per vestigia mandas
socium crucis ire latronem.   160

Patet ecce fidelibus ampli
via lucida iam paradisi,
licet et nemus illud adire,
homini quod ademerat anguis.

Illic precor, optime ductor,   165
famulam tibi praecipe mentem
genitali in sede sacrari,
quam liquerat exul et errans.

Nos tecta fovebimus ossa
violis et fronde frequenti,   170
titulumque et frigida saxa
liquido spargemus odore.

X. HYMN FOR THE BURIAL OF THE DEAD

Fountain of life, supernal Fire,
  Who didst unite in wondrous wise
  The soul that lives, the clay that dies,
And mad'st them Man: eternal Sire,

Both elements Thy will obey,
  Thine is the bond that joins the twain,
  And, while united they remain,
Spirit and body own Thy sway.

Yet they must one day disunite,
  Sunder in death this mortal frame;
  Dust to the dust from whence it came,
The spirit to its heavenward flight.

For all created things must wane,
  And age must break the bond at last;
  The diverse web that Life held fast
Death's fingers shall unweave again.

Yet, gracious God, Thou dost devise
  The death of Death for all Thine own;
  The path of safety Thou hast shown
Whereby the doomed limbs may rise:

So that, while fragile bonds of earth
  Man's noblest essence still enfold,
  That part may yet the sceptre hold
Which from pure aether hath its birth.

For if the earthy will hold sway,
  By gross desires and aims possessed,
  The soul, too, by the weight oppressed,
Follows the body's downward way.

But if she scorn the guilt that mars--
  Still mindful of her fiery sphere--
  She bears the flesh, her comrade here,
Back to her home beyond the stars.

The lifeless body we restore
  To earth, must slumber free from pain
  A little while, that it may gain
The spirit's fellowship once more.

The years will pass with rapid pace
  Till through these limbs the life shall flow,
  And the long-parted spirit go
To seek her olden dwelling-place.

Then shall the body, that hath lain
  And turned to dust in slow decay,
  On airy wings be borne away
And join its ancient soul again.

Therefore our tenderest care we spend
  Upon the grave: and mourners go

With solemn dirge and footstep slow--
Love's last sad tribute to a friend.

With fair white linen we enfold
  The dear dead limbs, and richest store
  Of Eastern unguents duly pour
Upon the body still and cold.

Why hew the rocky tomb so deep,
  Why raise the monument so fair,
  Save that the form we cherish there
Is no dead thing, but laid to sleep?

This is the faithful ministry
  Of Christian men, who hold it true
  That all shall one day live anew
Who now in icy slumber lie.

And he whose pitying hand shall lay
  Some friendless outcast 'neath the sod,
  E'en to the almighty Son of God
Doth that benignant service pay.

For this same law doth bid us mourn
  Man's common fate, when strangers die,
  And pay the tribute of a sigh,
As when our kin to rest are borne.

Of holy Tobit ye have read,
  (Grave father of a pious son),
  Who, though the feast was set, would run
To do his duty by the dead.

Though waiting servants stood around,
  From meat and drink he turned away
  And girt himself in haste to lay
The bones with weeping in the ground.

Soon Heaven his righteous zeal repays
  With rich reward; the eyes long blind
  In bitter gall strange virtue find
And open to the sun's clear rays.

Thus hath our Heavenly Father shown
  How sharp and bitter is the smart
  When sudden on the purblind heart
The Daystar's healing light is thrown.

He taught us, too, that none may gaze
  Upon the heavenly demesne
  Ere that in darkness and in pain
His feet have trod the world's rough ways.

So unto death itself is given
  Strange bliss, when mortal agony
  Opens the way that leads on high
And pain is but the path to Heaven.

Thus to a far serener day
  Our body from the grave returns;
  Eternal life within it burns
That knows nor languor nor decay.

These faces now so pinched and pale,
  That marks of lingering sickness show,
  Then fairer than the rose shall glow

And bloom with youth that ne'er shall fail.

Ne'er shall crabbed age their beauty dim
  With wrinkled brow and tresses grey,
  Nor arid leanness eat away
The vigour of the rounded limb.

Racked with his own destroying pains
  Shall fell Disease, who now attacks
  Our aching frames, his force relax
Fast fettered in a thousand chains:

While from its far celestial throne
  The immortal body, victor now,
  Shall watch its old tormentor bow
And in eternal tortures groan.

Why do the clamorous mourners wail
  In bootless sorrow murmuring?
  And why doth grief unreasoning
God's righteous ordinance assail?

Hushed be your voices, ye that mourn;
  Ye weeping mothers, dry the tear;
  Let none lament for children dear,
For man through Death to Life is born.

So do dry seeds grow green again,
  Now dead and buried in the earth,
  And rising to a second birth
Clothe as of old the verdant plain.

Take now, O earth, the load we bear,
  And cherish in thy gentle breast
  This mortal frame we lay to rest,
The poor remains that were so fair.

For they were once the soul's abode,
  That by God's breath created came;
  And in them, like a living flame,
Christ's precious gift of wisdom glowed.

Guard thou the body we have laid
  Within thy care, till He demand
  The creature fashioned by His hand
And after His own image made.

The appointed time soon may we see
  When God shall all our hopes fulfil,
  And thou must render to His will
Unchanged the charge we give to thee.

For though consumed by mould and rust
  Man's body slowly fades away,
  And years of lingering decay
Leave but a handful of dry dust;

Though wandering winds, that idly fly,
  Should his disparted ashes bear
  Through all the wide expanse of air,
Man may not perish utterly.

Yet till Thou dost build up again
  This mortal structure by Thy hand,
  In what far world wilt Thou command

The soul to rest, now free from stain?

In Abraham's bosom it shall dwell
  'Mid verdant bowers, as Lazarus lies
  Whom Dives sees with longing eyes
From out the far-off fires of hell.

We trust the words our Saviour said
  When, victor o'er grim Death, he cried
  To him who suffered at His side
"In Mine own footsteps shalt thou tread."

See, open to the faithful soul,
  The shining paths of Paradise;
  Now may they to that garden rise
Which from mankind the Serpent stole.

Guide him, we pray, to that blest bourn,
  Who served Thee truly here below;
  May he the bliss of Eden know,
Who strayed in banishment forlorn.

But we will honour our dear dead
  With violets and garlands strown,
  And o'er the cold and graven stone
Shall fragrant odours still be shed.

XI. HYMNUS VIII. KALENDAS IANUARIAS

Quid est, quod artum circulum
sol iam recurrens deserit?
Christusne terris nascitur,
qui lucis auget tramitem?

Heu quam fugacem gratiam   5
festina volvebat dies,
quam pene subductam facem
sensim recisa extinxerat!

Caelum nitescat laetius,
gratetur et gaudens humus,   10
scandit gradatim denuo
iubar priores lineas.

Emerge dulcis pusio,
quem mater edit castitas,
parens et expers coniugis,   15
mediator et duplex genus.

Ex ore quamlibet Patris
sis ortus et verbo editus,
tamen paterno in pectore
sophia callebas prius.   20

Quae prompta caelum condidit,
caelum diemque et cetera,
virtute verbi effecta sunt
haec cuncta: nam verbum Deus.

Sed ordinatis seculis,   25
rerumque digesto statu
fundator ipse et artifex
permansit in Patris sinu,

donec rotata annalium
transvolverentur milia,   30
atque ipse peccantem diu
dignatus orbera viseret.

Nam caeca vis mortalium
venerans inanes nenias
vel aera vel saxa algida,   35
vel ligna credebat Deum.

Haec dum sequuntur, perfidi
praedonis in ius venerant,
et mancipatam fumido
vitam barathro inmerserant: 40

Stragem sed istam non tulit
Christus cadentum gentium
inpune ne forsan sui
Patris periret fabrica.

Mortale corpus induit,   45
ut excitato corpore

mortis catenam frangeret
hominemque portaret Patri.

 Hic ille natalis dies,
quo te creator arduus   50
spiravit et limo indidit
sermone carnem glutinans.

 Sentisne, virgo nobilis,
matura per fastidia
pudoris intactum decus   55
honore partus crescere?

 O quanta rerum gaudia
alvus pudica continet,
ex qua novellum seculum
procedit et lux aurea!   60

 Vagitus ille exordium
vernantis orbis prodidit,
nam tunc renatus sordidum
mundus veternum depulit.

 Sparsisse tellurem reor   65
rus omne densis floribus,
ipsasque arenas syrtium
fragrasse nardo et nectare.

 Te cuncta nascentem puer
sensere dura et barbara,   70
victusque saxorum rigor
obduxit herbam cotibus.

Iam mella de scopulis fluunt,
iam stillat ilex arido
sudans amomum stipite,   75
iam sunt myricis balsama.

O sancta praesepis tui,
aeterne rex, cunabula,
populisque per seclum sacra
mutis et ipsis credita.   80

Adorat haec brutum pecus
indocta turba scilicet,
adorat excors natio,
vis cuius in pastu sita est.

Sed cum fideli spiritu   85
concurrat ad praesepia
pagana gens et quadrupes,
sapiatque quod brutum fuit:

Negat patrum prosapia
perosa praesentem Deum: 90
credas venenis ebriam
furiisve lymphatam rapi.

Quid prona per scelus ruis?
agnosce, si quidquam tibi
mentis resedit integrae,   95
ducem tuorum principum.

Hunc, quem latebra et obstetrix,
et virgo feta, et cunulae
et inbecilla infantia

regem dederunt gentibus,   100

  peccator intueberis
celsum coruscis nubibus,
deiectus ipse et inritus
plangens reatum fletibus:

  Cum vasta signum bucina   105
terris cremandis miserit,
et scissus axis cardinem
mundi ruentis solverit:

  Insignis ipse et praeminens
meritis rependet congrua,   110
his lucis usum perpetis,
illis gehennam et tartarum.

  Iudaea tunc fulmen crucis
experta, qui sit, senties,
quem te furoris praesule   115
mors hausit et mox reddidit.

XI. HYMN FOR CHRISTMAS-DAY

Why doth the sun re-orient take
A wider range, his limits break?
Lo! Christ is born, and o'er earth's night
Shineth from more to more the light!

Too swiftly did the radiant day
Her brief course run and pass away:
She scarce her kindly torch had fired
Ere slowly fading it expired.

Now let the sky more brightly beam,
The earth take up the joyous theme:
The orb a broadening pathway gains
And with its erstwhile splendour reigns.

Sweet babe, of chastity the flower,
A virgin's blest mysterious dower!
Rise in Thy twofold nature's might:
Rise, God and man to reunite!

Though by the Father's will above
Thou wert begot, the Son of Love,
Yet in His bosom Thou didst dwell,
Of Wisdom the eternal Well;

Wisdom, whereby the heavens were made
And light's foundations first were laid:
Creative Word! all flows from Thee!
The Word is God eternally.

For though with process of the suns
The ordered whole harmonious runs,
Still the Artificer Divine
Leaves not the Father's inmost shrine.

The rolling wheels of Time had passed
O'er their millennial journey vast,
Before in judgment clad He came
Unto the world long steeped in shame.

The purblind souls of mortals crass
Had trusted gods of stone and brass,
To things of nought their worship paid
And senseless blocks of wood obeyed.

And thus employed, they fell below
The sway of man's perfidious foe:
Plunged in the smoky sheer abyss
They sank bereft of their true bliss.

But that sore plight of ruined man
Christ's pity could not lightly scan:
Nor let God's building nobly wrought
Ingloriously be brought to nought.

He wrapped Him in our fleshly guise,
That from the tomb He might arise,
And man released from death's grim snare

Home to His Father's bosom bear.

This is the day of Thy dear birth,
The bridal of the heaven and earth,
When the Creator breathed on Thee
The breath of pure humanity.

Ah! glorious Maid, dost thou not guess
What guerdon thy chaste soul shall bless,
How by thy ripening pangs is bought
An honour greater than all thought?

O what a load of joy untold
Thy womb inviolate doth hold!
Of thee a golden age is born,
The brightness of the earth's new morn!

Hearken! doth not the infant's wail
The universal springtide hail?
For now the world re-born lays by
Its gloomy, frost-bound apathy.

Methinks in all her rustic bowers
The earth is spread with clustering flowers:
Odours of nard and nectar sweet
E'en o'er the sands of Syrtes fleet.

All places rough and deserts wild
Have felt from far Thy coming, Child:
Rocks to Thy gentle empire bow
And verdure clothes the mountain brow.

Sweet honey from the boulder leaps:
The sere and leafless oak-bough weeps
A strange rich attar: tamarisks too
Of balsam pure distil the dew.

Blessed for ever, cradle dear,
The lowly stall, the cavern drear!
Men to this shrine, Eternal King,
With dumb brutes adoration bring.

The ox and ass in homage low
Obedient to their Maker bow:
Bows too the unlearn'd heartless crowd
Whose minds the sensual feast doth cloud.

Though, by the faithful Spirit impelled,
Shepherds and brutes, unreasoning held,
Yea, folk that did in darkness dwell
Discern their God in His poor cell:

Yet children of the sacred race
Blindly abhor the Incarnate grace:
By philtres you might deem them lulled
Or by some bacchic phrenzy dulled.

Why headlong thus to ruin stride?
If aught of soundness in you bide,
Behold in Him the Lord divine
Of all your patriarchal line.

Mark you the dim-lit cave, the Maid,
The humble nurse, the cradle laid,
The helpless infancy forlorn:

Yet thus the Gentiles' King was born!

Ah sinner, thou shalt one day see
This Child in dreadful majesty,
See Him in glorious clouds descend,
While thou thy guilty heart shalt rend.

Vain all thy tears, when loud shall sound
The trump, when flames shall scorch the ground,
When from its hinge the cloven world
Is loosed, in horrid tumult hurled.

Then throned on high, the Judge of all
Shall mortals to their reckoning call:
To these shall grant the prize of light,
To those Gehenna's gloomy night.

Then, Israel, shalt thou learn at length
The Cross hath, as the lightning, strength:
Doomed by thy wrath, He now is Lord,
Whom Death once grasped but soon restored.

XII. HYMNUS EPIPHANIAE

Quicumque Christum quaeritis,
oculos in altum tollite,
illic licebit visere
signum perennis gloriae.

Haec stella, quae solis rotam   5
vincit decore ac lumine,
venisse terris nuntiat
cum carne terrestri Deum.

Non illa servit noctibus
secuta lunam menstruam,   10
sed sola caelum possidens
cursum dierum temperat.

Arctoa quamvis sidera
in se retortis motibus
obire nolint, attamen   15
plerumque sub nimbis latent.

Hoc sidus aeternum manet,
haec stella nunquam mergitur,
nec nubis occursu abdita
obumbrat obductam facem.   20

Tristis cometa intercidat,
et si quod astrum Sirio
fervet vapore, iam Dei
sub luce destructum cadat.

En Persici ex orbis sinu,   25
sol unde sumit ianuam,
cernunt periti interpretes
regale vexillum Magi.

Quod ut refulsit, ceteri
cessere signorum globi,   30
nec pulcher est ausus suam
conferre formam Lucifer.

Quis iste tantus, inquiunt,
regnator astris inperans,
quem sic tremunt caelestia,   35
cui lux et aethra inserviunt.

Inlustre quiddam cernimus,
quod nesciat finem pati,
sublime, celsum, interminum,
antiquius caelo et chao.   40

Hic ille rex est gentium
populique rex Iudaici,
promissus Abrahae patri
eiusque in aevum semini.

Aequanda nam stellis sua   45
cognovit olim germina

primus sator credentium,
nati inmolator unici.

Iam flos subit Davidicus
radice Iesse editus,   50
sceptrique per virgam virens
rerum cacumen occupat.

Exin sequuntur perciti
fixis in altum vultibus,
qua stella sulcum traxerat   55
claramque signabat viam.

Sed verticem pueri supra
signum pependit inminens,
pronaque submissum face
caput sacratum prodidit.   60

Videre quod postquam Magi,
eoa promunt munera,
stratique votis offerunt
tus, myrrham, et aurum regium.

Agnosce clara insignia   65
virtutis ac regni tui,
puer o, cui trinam Pater
praedestinavit indolem.

Regem Deumque adnuntiant
thesaurus et fragrans odor   70
turis Sabaei, ac myrrheus
pulvis sepulcrum praedocet.

Hoc est sepulcrum, quo Deus,
dum corpus extingui sinit
atque id sepultum suscitat,   75
mortis refregit carcerem.

O sola magnarum urbium
maior Bethlem, cui contigit
ducem salutis caelitus
incorporatum gignere.   80

Altrice te summo Patri
haeres creatur unicus,
homo ex tonantis spiritu
idemque sub membris Deus.

Hunc et prophetis testibus   85
isdemque signatoribus,
testator et sator iubet
adire regnum et cernere:

Regnum, quod ambit omnia
diva et marina et terrea   90
a solis ortu ad exitum
et tartara et caelum supra.

Audit tyrannus anxius
adesse regum principem,
qui nomen Israel regat   95
teneatque David regiam.

Exclamat amens nuntio,
successor instat, pellimur;
satelles i, ferrum rape,

perfunde cunas sanguine.　　100

　Mas omnis infans occidat,
scrutare nutricum sinus,
interque materna ubera
ensem cruentet pusio.

　Suspecta per Bethlem mihi　　105
puerperarum est omnium
fraus, ne qua furtim subtrahat
prolem virilis indolis.

　Transfigit ergo carnifex
mucrone districto furens　　110
effusa nuper corpora,
animasque rimatur novas.

　Locum minutis artubus
vix interemptor invenit,
quo plaga descendat patens　　115
iuguloque maior pugio est.

　O barbarum spectaculum!
inlisa cervix cautibus
spargit cerebrum lacteum
oculosque per vulnus vomit.　　120

　Aut in profundum palpitans
mersatur infans gurgitem,
cui subter artis faucibus
singultat unda et halitus.

Salvete flores martyrum, 125
quos lucis ipso in limine
Christi insecutor sustulit,
ceu turbo nascentes rosas.

Vos prima Christi victima,
grex inmolatorum tener, 130
aram ante ipsam simplices
palma et coronis luditis.

Quid proficit tantum nefas,
quid crimen Herodem iuvat?
unus tot inter funcra 135
inpune Christus tollitur.

Inter coaevi sanguinis
fluenta solus integer
ferrum, quod orbabat nurus,
partus fefellit virginis. 140

Sic stulta Pharaonis mali
edicta quondam fugerat
Christi figuram praeferens
Moyses, receptor civium.

Cautum et statutum ius erat, 145
quo non liceret matribus,
cum pondus alvi absolverent,
puerile pignus tollere.

Mens obstetricis sedulae
pie in tyrannum contumax 150
ad spem potentis gloriae

furata servat parvulum:

  Quem mox sacerdotem sibi
adsumpsit orbis conditor,
per quem notatam saxeis   155
legem tabellis traderet.

  Licetne Christum noscere
tanti per exemplum viri?
dux ille caeso Aegyptio
absolvit Israel iugo.   160

  At nos subactos iugiter
erroris inperio gravi
dux noster hoste saucio
mortis tenebris liberat.

  Hic expiatam fluctibus   165
plebem marino in transitu
repurgat undis dulcibus,
lucis columnam praeferens:

  Hic praeliante exercitu,
pansis in altum brachiis,   170
sublimis Amalech premit,
crucis quod instar tunc fuit.

  Hic nempe Iesus verior,
qui longa post dispendia
victor suis tribulibus   175
promissa solvit iugera.

Qui ter quaternas denique
refluentis amnis alveo
fundavit et fixit petras,
apostolorum stemmata.   180

Iure ergo se Iudae ducem
vidisse testantur Magi,
cum facta priscorum ducum
Christi figuram finxerint.

Hic rex priorum iudicum,   185
rexere qui Iacob genus,
dominaeque rex ecclesiac,
templi et novelli et pristini.

Hunc posteri Efrem colunt,
hunc sancta Manasse domus   190
omnesque suspiciunt tribus
bis sena fratrum semina.

Quin et propago degener
ritum secuta inconditum,
quaecumque dirum fervidis   195
Baal caminis coxerat,

fumosa avorum numina
saxum, metallum, stipitem,
rasum, dolatum, sectile,
in Christi honorem deserit.   200

Gaudete quidquid gentium est,
Iudaea, Roma, et Graecia,
Aegypte, Thrax, Persa, Scytha,

rex unus omnes possidet.

  Laudate vestrum principem   205
omnes beati, ac perditi,
vivi, inbecilli ac mortui:
iam nemo posthac mortuus.

XII. HYMN FOR THE EPIPHANY

Lift up your eyes, whoe'er ye be
That fare the new-born Christ to see:
For yonder is the shining sign
Of grace perennial and divine.

What means this star, whose piercing rays
Outshine the sun's resplendent blaze?
'Tis token sure that God is come
In mortal flesh to make His home.

No courtier of the realms of night
Nor monthly moon's bright acolyte,
This star directs the course of day,
Sole sovereign of the heavenly way.

Although the Bears their track retrace,
Nor wholly their clear beams efface,
Yet ofttimes 'neath the dun cloud's haze
They hide themselves from mortal gaze.

But yon Star's glory hath no end,
Nor to the depths can it descend:
It ne'er is whelmed by envious cloud
That seeks its beauty to enshroud.

Now let the baleful comet die,
The brood of blazing Sirius fly:
God's orb shall quench their sultry heats
And drive them from their haughty seats.

Lo! from the regions of the morn
Wherein the radiant sun is born,
The Persian sages see on high
God's ensign shining in the sky.

Soon as its rising beams prevail
The starry hosts in order pale:
E'en Lucifer durst not upraise
The silvery splendours of his face.

Who is this sovereign (they enquire)
That lords it o'er the ethereal choir?
'Fore whom the heavens bow down afraid,
Of all the worlds of light obeyed?

Sure 'tis the sign most reverend
Of Being that doth know no end:
Of One in state sublime arrayed
Ere sky and chaos yet were made.

This is the King of Israel,
Of all in Gentile lands that dwell:
The King to Abram and his seed
Throughout all ages erst decreed.

To him 'twas given his progeny
As stars innumerous to see:
First of believers! moved to slay

His only son, so God to obey.

Behold the Flower of David shine,
Of Jesse's root the Branch benign:
The sceptre spread with blossoms rare
Wields o'er the world its lordship fair.

Roused by the portent of the sky
The sages fix their gaze on high,
And speed them 'neath the furrowed way
Marked by the star's effulgent ray.

At length its flaming steps it stayed
Poised over where the Child was laid:
Straightway with downcast mien it shed
Its splendours on the sacred Head.

Whereat the travellers outpour
Of Eastern gifts their treasure-store,
Myrrh and sweet-smelling frankincense,
Gold meet for regal opulence.

Behold herein the triple sign
Of Thy pure being, King divine:
Seeing the Father willed in Thee
To plant a threefold majesty.

The gift of gold thee King proclaims:
Thee God the fragrant incense names:
The myrrh declares that Death shall thrust
Within the tomb Thy body's dust.

Ah! that dark sepulchre, whose fold
God's body quenched in death doth hold:
Yet shall He from that durance wake
And Death's strong prison-fetters break.

O Bethlehem! no longer thou
The least of cities: all shall vow
That thou art greatest on the earth:
For thou man's King didst bring to birth.

Yea thou didst on thy bosom bear
The All-loving Father's only heir:
Man of the Thunderer's Spirit made
And God in human flesh arrayed.

The prophets witnessed to the bond
Which sealed to Him the realm profound:
The Father's Kingdom He received
And the vast legacy perceived.

All things are His in sea and sky,
In hell beneath, in heaven on high:
From East to setting sun, in fee
He holds the earth's immensity.

Distraught, the tyrant base doth hear
That now the King of Kings draws near
To reign in David's seat of state
And Israel's empire dominate.

"Betrayed are we," he maddened cries,
"Our throne's usurper doth arise:
Go, soldiers, go with sword in hand

And slay all babes within my land.

"Spare no male child: each nurse's robe
Your scrutizing steel must probe:
Spare not the suckling infant, though
O'er mother's breast its life-blood flow.

"On Bethlehem our suspicion falls,
On every hearth within its walls:
Lest mothers with love's tender zeal
Some manly scion may conceal."

With daggers drawn the infuriate crew
Upon their murderous errand flew:
Each latest offspring of the womb
To bloody death they foully doom.

Ah tiny limbs! 'twas hard to know
How best to strike the fatal blow:
Too wide the sword-blades are to smite
Those throats so silken-fragile, slight.

O horrid sight! the tender bones
Are dashed against the jagged stones:
Sightless and mangled there they lie,
Poor babes! untimely doomed to die.

Perchance the still deep river laves
Their bodies thrust into the waves:
The current with their sighing sighs,
Sobs with their latest, broken cries.

Ye flowers of martyrdom, all hail!
Of rising morn pure blossoms frail!
By Jesu's foe were ye downcast,
Like budding roses by the blast.

Lambs of the flock too early slain,
Ye first fruits of Christ's bitter pain!
Close to His very altar, gay
With palms and crowns, ye now do play.

Of what avail is deed so vile?
Doth Herod gain by murderous guile?
Of all to death so foully done
Escapes triumphant Christ alone.

Amidst that tide of infant gore
Alone He wins the sheltering shore:
The virgin's Child survives the stroke,
When every mother's heart was broke.

Thus Moses 'scaped the mad decree
Of evil Pharaoh and set free
The flock of God, prefiguring so
Christ spared from fate's malignant blow.

Vain too the king's hostility
Who framed the pitiless decree
That Israel's mothers should not rear
To manhood's strength their offspring dear.

Quickened by love, a woman's mind
Found means to thwart that law unkind,
And, falsely true, the child concealed

Destined to be his people's Shield.

On him it was that God did place
The august priesthood's holy grace,
The law on stony tablets writ
Did to his trembling hands commit.

And may we not with prophet's eye
In such a hero Christ descry?
The proud Egyptian's might he broke
And freed his kinsmen from the yoke.

So we by Error's might hemmed round
Were by our Captain's strength unbound:
His foe He wounded in the fight
And saved us from Death's horrid night.

Cheering by sign of flame their feet,
Moses renewed with waters sweet
His folk, albeit purified
From stain, what time they crossed the tide.

And he, remote on peaceful height,
Amalek's banded hosts did smite:
He prayed with arms stretched out above,
Foreshadowing the Cross of Love.

Yet truer Jesus surely he,
Who after many a victory
And labours long the tribes' renown
With promised heritage did crown;

Who when the waters rose on high
And now the Jordan's bed was dry,
Set up twelve stones of memory,
Types of apostles yet to be.

Rightly the Wise Men said, I ween,
That they Judaea's King had seen,
Since noble deeds of other days
Prophetic chant the Saviour's praise.

Of those old rulers He is King
Who did to Jacob judgment bring,
King of the Mother Church divine,
God's ancient and God's present Shrine.

Of Ephraim's sons He is adored:
Manasseh's sacred house as Lord
Reveres Him: to His might the seed
Of brethren twelve their fealty plead.

Nay, each degenerate race hath fled
Its shameful rites and orgies dread:
Grim Baal in glowing furnace cast
Sinks to the earth, forsook at last.

Idols smoke-blackened, wooden-hewn,
Of brass and stone, in dust are strewn:
The chiselled deities downtrod:
For all confess in Christ their God.

Rejoice all peoples, Jewry, Rome,
Fair Hellas, Thrace, Aegyptus' home:
Persians and Scythian land forlorn,

Rejoice: the world's great King is born!

Behold your Chief! His praise forth tell:
Ye sick, ye hale, all heaven and hell:
Ay, you whose vital spark hath sped:
For lo! in Him e'en Death is dead.

EPILOGUS

Inmolat Deo Patri
  pius, fidelis, innocens, pudicus
dona conscientiae,
  quibus beata mens abundat intus:
alter et pecuniam   5
  recidit, unde victitent egeni.
Nos citos iambicos
  sacramus et rotatiles trochaeos,
sanctitatis indigi
  nec ad levamen pauperum potentes;   10
adprobat tamen Deus
  pedestre carmen, et benignus audit.
Multa divitis domo
  sita est per omnes angulos supellex.
Fulget aureus scyphus,   15
  nec aere defit expolita pelvis:
est et olla fictilis,
  gravisque et ampla argentea est parabsis.
Sunt eburna quaepiam,
  nonnulla quercu sunt cavata et ulmo: 20
omne vas fit utile,
  quod est ad usum congruens herilem,
Instruunt enim domum
  ut empta magno, sic parata ligno.

Me paterno in atrio 25
  ut obsoletum vasculum caducis
Christus aptat usibus,
  sinitque parte in anguli manere.
Munus ecce fictile
  inimus intra regiam salutis; 30
attamen vel infimam
  Deo obsequelam praestitisse prodest.
Quidquid illud accidit,
  iuvabit ore personasse Christum.

EPILOGUE

The pure and faithful saint, whose heart is whole,
  To God the Father makes his sacrifice
From out the treasures of a stainless soul,
  Glad gifts of innocence, beyond all price:
Another with free hand bestows his gold,
  Whereby his needy neighbour may be fed.
No wealth of holiness my heart doth hold,
  No store have I to buy my brothers bread:
So here I humbly dedicate to Thee
  The rolling trochee and iambus swift;
Thou wilt approve my simple minstrelsy,
  Thine ear will listen to Thy servant's gift.
The rich man's halls are nobly furnished;
  Therein no nook or corner empty seems;
Here stands the brazen laver burnished,
  And there the golden goblet brightly gleams;
Hard by some crock of clumsy earthen ware,
  Massive and ample lies a silver plate;
And rough-hewn cups of oak or elm are there
  With vases carved of ivory delicate.
Yet every vessel in its place is good,
  So be it for the Master's service meet;
The priceless salver and the bowl of wood
  Alike He needs to make His home complete.

Therefore within His Father's spacious hall
  Christ fits me for the service of a day,
Mean though I be, a vessel poor and small,--
  And in some lowly corner lets me stay.
Lo in the palace of the King of Kings
  I play the earthen pitcher's humble part;
Yet to have done Him meanest service brings
  A thrill of rapture to my thankful heart:
Whate'er the end, this thought will joy afford,
  My lips have sung the praises of my Lord.

This edition of the ***Cathemerinon of Prudentius*** has been prepared for the Temple Classics by Rev. R. MARTIN POPE, M.A. (St John's College, Cambridge, translator of the "Letters of John Hus"), who has done the translation of the ***Praefatio*** and Hymns i., ii., iii., viii., xi., xii., with notes thereon and the note on ***Prudentius.*** For the rendering of ***Hymns iv., v., vi., vii., ix., x.,*** and the ***Epilogus*** with notes thereon, Mr R.F. DAVIS, M.A. (St John's College, Cambridge), is responsible. The text, with some minor alterations in orthography and punctuation, is that of Dressel (Lipsiae, 1860). The frontispiece is due to the kind suggestion of ***Dr SANDYS,*** Public Orator of Cambridge University, to whom the thanks of the translators are hereby presented.

TRANSLATOR'S NOTE

AURELIUS PRUDENTIUS CLEMENS (to give his full title) was born, probably at Saragossa (Caesaraugusta), in Spain, in the year of our Lord 348. The fourth century exercised a profound influence alike on the destiny of the Roman Empire and of the Christian Church. After a long discipline, strangely alternating between fiery persecution and contemptuous toleration, the Church entered upon a new era, when in 323 Constantine, the first Christian emperor, became master of the Roman world. Two years later the Council of Nicaea met to utter its verdict on the Arian controversy and to establish the terms of the orthodox symbol. A generation later Julian took up the reins of empire and commenced his quixotic and fruitless attempt to revive the glories of Paganism. Athanasius died in 373: but fourteen years later Augustine, his successor in the championship of the faith, was baptized, and in 395, at the death of Theodosius, when the Empire was divided between Honorius and Arcadius, he became Bishop of Hippo, and was marked out by his saintliness and learning as the leader of the Western Church, which he shaped by his splendid ideal of the *Civitas Dei* into unity and stability, when the secular empire was falling into decay.

We know little more of the life of Prudentius than he himself has disclosed. The *Preface*, which stands as an introduction to his poems, is a miniature autobiography of great interest. M. Boissier in his *Fin du Paganisme* ***calls it*** melancolique : though it is rather the retrospect of a serious and awakened, but not morbid, conscience. Prudentius views his past years in the light of that new spiritual truth to which he has opened his soul. We gather that he received a liberal education and was called to the bar. We need not misunderstand the allusion to the deceitfulness of the barrister life, seeing that the ordinary arts of rhetoric stand condemned by his recently adopted ethical standard. He held two important judicial posts and was promoted to a high position, probably in the civil service and not outside the limits of his native province, the provincia Tarraconensis.

He speaks of himself as having reached the age of fifty-seven, which brings us down to 405, and as intending to consecrate his remaining years to the poetic treatment of religious subjects. When and how he became a Christian we do not know, and it were vain to guess, although the suggestion that he may have owed his conversion to the influence of some Christian family of his acquaintance is at least interesting. It is unlikely that he took up poetry for the first time in his old age. His mastery of all kinds of metre--heroic and lyric--prove the practised hand. The probability is that in the years of repose after a busy career his desire to redeem an unspiritual past suggested for the exercise of his natural gifts a field hitherto unoccupied by any of the writers of his age. Why not consecrate his powers to the task of interesting the literary circles of the Empire in the evangel of Christ? Why not present the truths of Christianity in a poetic guise, wrought into forms of beauty and set forth in the classical metres of Roman literature? This became the passion of his life, and however we may view the results of his toil, the spirit in which he went to work, as described in the touching Epilogue, cannot but evoke our profound admiration. He is but a vessel of earth, but whatever the issue may be, it will be a lasting joy to have sounded forth the praise of Christ in song.

This then is how Prudentius becomes the first poet of the Christian Church, or, as Bentley called him, "the Virgil and Horace of the Christians." Doubtless there were other influences at work to determine the sphere to which he was naturally attract. Ambrose, who was Bishop of Milan when Prudentius was twenty-six years of age, had written the first Latin hymns to be sung in church. Augustine in a familiar passage of the Confessions (ix. 7.) describes how "the custom arose of singing hymns and psalms, after the use of the Eastern provinces, to save the people from being utterly worn out by their long and sorrowful vigils." "From that day to this," he adds, "it has been retained and, many might say, all Thy flocks throughout the rest of the world now follow our example." To Ambrose and Augustine the Church of Christ is for ever indebted: to the latter for a devotional treatise which is the most familiar of all the writings of the fourth century: to the former for the hymns of praise which he composed and the practice of singing which he thus inaugurated in the worship of the Western Church. But the Church owes something also to Prudentius, a much more gifted poet than Ambrose. The collection of hymns known as the Cathemerinon *or* Hymns for the day is as little adapted for ecclesiastical worship as Keble's Christian Year, although excerpts from these poems have passed into the hymnology of the Church, just as portions of Keble's work have passed into most hymn books. For example, seven of these excerpts in the form of hymns are to be found in the Roman Breviary, and thus for centuries the lyrics of Prudentius have been sung in the daily services of the Church.

Seeing that Prudentius must address himself to most English readers through the imperfect medium of a translation, it may be well to remind those who make their first acquaintance with him that a historical imagination is an indispensable condition of interest and sympathy. If Prudentius has a habit of leaving the main issue and making lengthy and tedious detours into the picturesque parables and miraculous incidents of the Old Testament, there is method in his digressiveness. He knows that one of the charms of Paganism lies in its rich and variegated mythology. Yet Christianity also can point to an even nobler inheritance of the supernatural and the wonderful in the mysterious evolutions of its history. Hence the stories of the early patriarchs, of the Israelites and Moses, of Daniel and Jonah, are imported by the poet as pictorial illustrations of his theme. If occasionally the details border on the grotesque, he certainly reveals a striking knowledge of the Old Testament.

The New Testament is also adequately represented. In one poem (ix.) the miracles of Christ in His earthly ministry and His descent into Hades are narrated with considerable spirit and eloquence. Besides being a student of the Bible, Prudentius is a theologian. His theology is that of the Nicene Creed. The Fall of man, the personality of the Tempter, the mystery of the Trinity and of the Incarnation, the Virgin-birth, the Death and Resurrection of Christ, the pains of the lost and the bliss of the saints, the resurrection of the Body and the life everlasting--these are the themes of his pen, the themes too of the theology of his age. If the poet's treatment of these truths occasionally appears antiquated and crude to modern ideas, it is at least dignified and intelligent. His mind has absorbed the Christian religion and the Christian theology, and he not unfrequently rises to noble heights in the interpretation of their mysteries. His didactic poems, the Hamartigenia **or the** Origin of Evil and the Apotheosis, a treatise on the Person of Christ, prove him to be a theologian of no mean calibre. He is also an allegorist, as is proved by the Psychomachia **or the** Battle of the Soul, a kind of Holy War which was very popular in the Middle Ages. He is a martyrologist: as witness the Peristephanon, a series of poems on Christian, principally Spanish, martyrs. Moreover, he is an undoubted patriot, and in the Contra Symmachum, which he wrote on the famous affair of the Altar of Victory, he proves that, while a Christian, he is also civis Romanus, loyal to the Empire and the powers that be. He is a skilful versifier, and in this connection the quatrains of the Dittochaeon, verses on themes of the Old and New Testaments, may be mentioned in order to complete the list of his works. His mastery of his very varied metres--hexameter, iambic, trochaic and sapphic--is undoubted: everywhere we note the influence of Virgil and Horace, even when these poets are not recalled by echoes of their diction which are constantly greeting the reader of his poems.

Reference has already been made to the influence of Ambrose of Milan upon the thought and style of Prudentius. But there is a second and even more powerful influence that deserves at least briefly to be noted--namely, the Christian art of the Catacombs. Apart from such definite statements as e.g. *are found in* Peristephanon xi., it is obvious that Prudentius had a first-hand knowledge of Rome and particularly of the Catacombs. Everywhere in his poems we find evidences of the deep impression made upon his imagination by the paintings and sculptures of subterranean Rome. The now familiar representations which decorate the remains of the Catacombs suggested to him many of the allusions, the picturesque vignettes and glowing descriptions to be found in his poetry. Thus, the story of Jonah--a common theme typifying the Resurrection--the story of Daniel with its obvious consolations for an age of martyrs, the Good Shepherd and the denial of Peter may be mentioned among the numerous subjects which were reproduced in early Christian art and transferred by the poet to his verse. The symbolism of the Cock, the Dove, and the Lamb borne on the shoulders of the Good Shepherd is a perpetually recurring feature in the lyrics and martyr-hymns of Prudentius, who thus becomes one of our most valuable authorities on the Christian art of the fourth century.

The poems, of which a new English rendering is presented in this volume, are acknowledged by most critics to illustrate some of his best qualities, his brightness and dignity, his touches of nature-painting and his capacity for sustained and well-wrought narrative. As we study these lyrics of the early Church, we feel anew the mighty change that Christianity wrought in Roman life by its doctrine of immortality, and we note the curious fascination which the circumstances of the Nativity and especially the Adoration of the Magi had for the Western world. Prudentius had a great vogue in the Middle Ages, and the modern renewal of interest in mediaevalism invests with fresh dignity a poet whose works at the Revival of learning provoked the admiration of Erasmus[1] and the researches of numerous scholars and editors. But it is undoubtedly to the student of

1   Prudentium, unum inter Christianos vere facundum poetam.

ecclesiastical history and dogma and to the lovers of Christian art and antiquities that Prudentius most truly appeals. He claims our interest, not merely because he reflects the Christian environment of his days, but because his poetry represents an attempt to preach Christ to a world still fascinated by Paganism, while conscious that the old order was changing and yielding place to new.

NOTES
HYMNS

THE TITLE

The word Cathemerinon is taken from the Greek and is the genitive of chathemerina *"daily things": the whole title* Liber Cathemerinon is equivalent to "Book of daily hymns," and may be rendered "Hymns for the Christian's day."

THE PREFACE

In one or two of the MSS. this introductory poem is stated to be a preface of the Cathemerinon only: but the great majority of the codices support the view which is undoubtedly suggested by internal evidence, that the poem is a general introduction to the whole of Prudentius' works. It is inserted together with the Epilogus in this volume, because of the intrinsic interest of both poems.

Line

8   The reference is to the toga virilis, the ordinary white-coloured garb of a Roman citizen who at his sixteenth year laid aside the purple-edged toga praetexta, which was worn during the days of boyhood.

16 ff.   The cities referred to are unknown: but it is probable that
they were two municipia in Northern Spain, and that the office
held by Prudentius was that of duumvir or prefect. Provision was made
by the twenty-fourth clause of the law of Salpensa (a town in the
provincia Baetica of Spain) by which the emperor could be elected
first magistrate of a municipium, and could thereupon appoint a
prefect to take his place. This would explain the language of the
text as to the semi-imperial nature of the post. The phrase
militiae gradus need only be taken to indicate advancement in the
civil service. But the words have been interpreted in accordance
with the more familiar and definite meaning of militia, and
understood to refer to a purely military post. Dressel thinks that
Prudentius was a miles Palatinus, that is, a member of the
best-paid and most highly-privileged imperial troops, who furnished
officers for some of the most lucrative posts in the provinces.
Though in the translation the usual meaning has been given to
militia, it must be regarded as uncertain in the absence of
more definite information regarding the office held by Prudentius.

24   The consulship of Salia (or Salias) belongs to the year 348, the
date of the birth of Prudentius. An inscription (quoted by Migne from
Muratorius, Nov. Thes. Inscrip., i. 379) has been found in the
monastery of St. Paul's outside the city bearing the words

FILIPPO . ET . SALLIA . COSS

I

1 Of this poem lines 1-8, 81-84, 97-100, were included in the Roman Breviary as a hymn to be sung at Lauds, on Tuesday.

2 The allusions to the cock in this and the following poem (ii. 37-55) were doubtless inspired by the lines of Ambrose in his morning hymn beginning Aeterne rerum conditor. Cf. ll. 5-8 and 16-24:

> "praeco diei iam sonat
> noctis profundae pervigil,
> nocturna lux viantibus
> a nocte noctem segregans.

> *   *   *   *   *

> surgamus ergo strenue:
> gallus iacentes excitat,
> et somnolentos increpat:
> gallus negantes arguit.

> gallo canente spes redit,
> aegris salus refunditur,
> mucro latronis conditur,
> lapsis fides revertitur."

Translation.

"Dawn's herald now begins to cry,
Lone watcher of the nightly sky:

Light of the dark to pilgrims dear,
Speeding successive midnights drear.

*   *   *   *   *

Brisk from our couch let us arise!
Hark to the cock's arousing cries!
He chides the sluggard's slumbrous ease,
And shames his unconvincing pleas.

At cock-crow Hope revives again,
Health banishes the stress of pain,
Sheathed is the nightly robber's sword,
And Faith to fallen hearts restored."

See also Ambrose, Hexaem., v. 24, for an eloquent passage in
the same strain. The cock was the familiar Christian symbol of early
rising or vigilance, and numerous representations of it are found in
the Catacombs. Cf. the painting from the Catacomb of St. Priscilla
reproduced in Bottari's folio of 1754, where the Good Shepherd is
depicted as feeding the lambs, with a crowing cock on His right and
left hand. It is also a symbol of the Resurrection, our Lord being
supposed to have risen from the grave at the early cockcrowing: see
l. 65 et seq. In l. 16 the first bird-notes are interpreted
by the poet as a summons to the general judgment. Cf. Mark xiii. 35:
"Ye know not when the lord of the house cometh, whether at even, or
at midnight, or at cockcrowing, or in the morning." This
passage serves as a kind of text for Prudentius' first two hymns,
and perhaps explains why he has one for cockcrowing and another for
morning.

26   A common idea in all literatures. Cf. Virg., Aen., vi. 278

(taken from Homer), tum consanguineus Leti Sopor, and Tennyson's "Sleep, Death's twin-brother" (In Memoriam, 68).

44   Cf. Augustine, Serm. 103: "These evil spirits seek to seduce the soul: but when the sun has arisen, they take to flight."

59   The denial of Peter forms a subject of Christian casuistry in patristic literature, and this passage recalls the famous classical parallel in Euripides (Hipp. 612), "the tongue hath sworn: yet unsworn is the heart." Cf. Augustine, cont. mendacium: "In that denial he held fast the truth in his heart, while with his lips he uttered falsehood." For a striking representation of Peter and the cock, on a sarcophagus discovered in the Catacombs and now deposited in the Vatican library, see Maitland's Church in the Catacombs, p. 347. The closing words of the passage in Ambrose's Hexaemeron, already referred to under l. 2, may here be quoted: "As the cock peals forth his notes, the robber leaves his plots: Lucifer himself awakes and lights up the sky: the distressful sailor lays aside his gloom, and all the storms and tempests that have risen in fury under the winds of the evening begin to die down: the soul of the saint leaps to prayer and renews the study of the written word: and finally, the very Rock of the Church is cleansed of the stain he had contracted by his denials before the cock crew."

81 ff.   The best commentary on these words is to be found in the following passage from the second epistle of Basil to Gregory Nazianzen: "What can be more blessed than to imitate on earth the angelic host by giving oneself at the peep of dawn to prayer and by turning at sunrise to work with hymns and songs: yea, all the day through to make prayer the accompaniment of our toils and to season them with praise as with salt? For the solace of hymns changes the soul's sadness into mirth."

II

1   This poem furnishes two hymns to the Roman Breviary, one to be sung
on Wednesday at Lauds, and consisting of ll. 1-8, 48-53 (omitting l.
50), 57, 59, 60, 67 (tu vera lux caelestium) and 68: the other
for Thursday at Lauds, consisting of ll. 25 (lux ecce surgit
aurea), 93-108.

17   Cf. Ambrose, ii. 8, de Cain et Abel: "The thief shuns the day
as the witness of his crime: the adulterer is abashed by the dawn
as the accomplice of his adultery."

51   The practice of praying on bended knees is frequently referred to
in early Christian writers. Cf. Clem., 1 Ad. Cor. cc. xlviii.: "Let
us fall down before the Lord," and Shepherd of Hermas, vis. 1. i.:
"After I had crossed that river I came unto the banks and there
knelt down and began to pray." Dressel quotes from Juvencus (iv.
648), a Spanish poet and Christian contemporary of Prudentius,
genibus nixi regem dominumque salutant, "on bended knees they
make obeisance unto their King and Lord."

63   The Jordan is a poetical figure for baptism, suggested doubtless
by the baptism of our Lord in that river. Cf. vii. 73-75.

67   Cf. Milton, Paradise Regained, i. 293: "So spake our Morning
Star, then in his rise." The figure is suggested by Rev. xxii. 16:
"I am ... the bright, the morning star."

105   The conception of God as speculator may be paralleled by a
passage in the epistle of Polycarp ad Philipp. iv., where God is
described as the Arch-critic (panta momoschopeitai) and subsequently
(vii.) as ton pantepopten theon, "the All-witnessing God." The

last verse contains a distinct echo of the closing words of the
fourth chapter of Polycarp: "None of the reasonings or thoughts,
nor any of the hidden things of the heart escape His notice."

III

2   Word-begot. ***The original*** verbigena, on the analogy of such
words (cf. terrigena, Martigena, etc.), can only mean "begotten
of the Word." It is evident, therefore, the "Word" in this connection
is not the Johannine Logos or Second Person in the Trinity.
Prudentius cannot be guilty of the error which he expressly
condemns (Apoth. 249) as perquam ridiculum and regard the
Logos as begetting Himself. Consequently, both in this passage and
in xi. 18 (verbo editus) the "Word" must be taken as approximating
rather to the Alexandrian conception of the Logos as the Divine
Reason. In this way Christ is expressly described as the offspring
of the Intellectus Dei, the immanent Intelligence of the Deity.
If this conception is considered to be beyond Prudentius, we can only
suppose that both here and in xi. 18, his language is theologically
loose. Some excuse may be offered for this on the ground that the
Latin language is ill-adapted for expressing metaphysical truths.
The late Bishop Westcott remarked on the inadequacy of the Latin
original of "the Word was made flesh" (verbum caro factum est),
both substantive and verb falling short of the richness of their
Greek equivalents. (Vid. also note on iv. 15.)

11   Cf. Ambrose, Hymn vii.:--

"Christusque nobis sit cibus
Potusque noster sit fides;
Laeti bibamus sobriam
Ebrietatem Spiritus."

Translation.

"May Christ be now the Bread we eat,
Be simple Faith our potion sweet:
Let our intoxication be
The Spirit's calm sobriety."

The idea is familiar to readers of Herbert and Herrick, though it
is elaborated by them with quaint conceits somewhat foreign to the
Latin poet. Cf. Herbert, The Banquet :--

"O what sweetnesse from the bowl
    Fills my soul!

          *   *   *   *   *

Is some starre (fled from the sphere)
    Melted there,
As we sugar melt in wine?

          *   *   *   *   *

Doubtless neither starre nor flower
    Hath the power
Such a sweetnesse to impart:
Only God, Who gives perfumes,
    Flesh assumes,
And with it perfumed my heart."

Also Herrick, A Thanksgiving to God :--

"Lord, I confess too, when I dine,
      The pulse is thine.

         *   *   *   *   *

'Tis thou that crown'st my glittering hearth
      With guiltless mirth,
And giv'st me wassail bowls to drink,
      Spiced to the brink."

28   The original dactylico refers to the metre of the Latin of this
     poem. For a rendering of ll. 1-65 in the metre of the original see
     Glover, Life and Letters in the Fourth Century, pp. 267-269.

58   This and the following lines should satisfy the most ardent
     vegetarian who seeks to uphold his abstinence from animal food by
     the customs of the early Church. In Christian circles, however, the
     abstinence was practised on personal and spiritual grounds, e.g.,
     Jerome (de Regul. Monach., xi.) says, "The eating of flesh is the
     seed-plot of lust" (seminarium libidinis): so also Augustine (de
     moribus Ecc. Cath., i. 33), who supports what doubtless was the
     view of Prudentius, namely that the avoidance of animal flesh was a
     safe-guard but not a binding Christian duty.

75   Unwed. Prudentius thus adopts the view of the ancient world on
     the question of the generation of bees. Cf. Virgil, Geo. iv. 198,
     and Pliny, Nat. Hist., xi. 16. Dryden's translation of Virgil
     (l.c.) is as follows:--

     "But (what's more strange) their modest appetites,
     Averse from Venus, fly the nuptial rights;
     No lust enervates their heroic mind,

Nor wastes their strength on wanton womankind,
But in their mouths reside their genial powers,
They gather children from the leaves and flowers."

86   Cf. Ps. liv. 18, 19 (Vulg.): Vespere et mane et meridie narrabo
et annuntiabo et exaudiet vocem meam. "In the evening and morning
and at noonday will I pray, and that instantly and he shall hear my
voice" (P. B. Version).

127   This is, strictly speaking, an error: it is the woman's seed
which is to bruise the serpent's head. The error was perpetuated
in the Latin Church by the Vulgate of Gen. iii. 15, ipsa conteret
caput tuum, where ipsa refers to the woman (= she herself).

157   The epithet "white-robed" refers to the newly-baptized converts
who received the white robe as a symbol of their new nature. Cf.
Perist. *i. 67:* Christus illic candidatis praesidet cohortibus,
and Ambrose (de Mysteriis, vii.): "Thou didst receive (that is,
after baptism) white garments as a sign that thou hast doffed the
covering of thy sins and put on the chaste raiment (velamina) of
innocence, whereof the prophet spake (Ps. li. 7), 'Thou shalt purge
me with hyssop, and I shall be clean: thou shalt wash me, and I
shall be whiter than snow'" (Vulg.).

199   Phlegethon (rendered "Hell"), one of the rivers of the Virgilian
Hades, is used to express the abode of the lost. Cf. Milton, P. L.,
ii. 580:--

       "... fierce Phlegethon,
   Whose waves of torrent fire inflame with rage."

The subject of the descensus ad inferos was evidently a favourite
one with Prudentius and his contemporaries. It has been suggested

that apart from the scriptural basis of this conception Prudentius
was influenced by the so-called Gospel of Nicodemus, which embodies
two books, the Acts of Pilate **and the** Descent into Hell. The
latter is assigned by several critics to 400 or thereabouts, and
gives a graphic account of Christ's doings in Hades. Synesius deals
with the subject in one of his hymns (ix.), and Mrs Browning's
translation (see the essay on The Greek Christian Poets) of a
passage in that poem may be quoted:--

"Down Thou earnest, low as earth,
Bound to those of mortal birth;
Down Thou earnest, low as hell,
Where Shepherd-Death did tend and keep
A thousand nations like to sheep,
While weak with age old Hades fell
Shivering through his dark to view Thee.

*   *   *   *   *

So, redeeming from their pain
Chains of disembodied ones,
Thou didst lead whom thou didst gather
Upward in ascent again,
With a great hymn to the Father,
Upward to the pure white thrones!"

For a modern treatment of the theme see Christ in Hades, by
Stephen Phillips.

202   The words suggest the Catacombs, and perhaps refer to the custom
of placing in the tomb a small cup or vase containing spices, of
which myrrh (a symbol of death, according to Gregory of Nyssa, cf.

xii. 71) was most usually employed. Or the allusion may be to the practice of embalming. (See note on x. 51.) The body was placed not only in an actual sarcophagus or stone coffin, as expressly mentioned in the text, but in hollow places cut out of rock or earth (loculus). The sarcophagus method seems to have been the earlier, but was superseded by that of the loculus, except in the case of the very wealthy.

205   The concluding line is beautifully illustrated by the epitaph on the martyr Alexander, found over one of the graves in the cemetery of Callixtus in the Catacombs:--

ALEXANDER MORTVVS NON EST SED VIVIT
SVPER ASTRA ET CORPVS IN HOC TVMVLO
QVIESCIT ...

"Alexander is not dead, but lives above the stars
    and his body rests in this tomb."

IV

15   Prudentius here, as again in v. 160, emphasises his belief in the procession of the Holy Ghost from the Father and the Son. The "filioque" clause was not actually added to the Nicene Creed till the Council of Toledo (589 A.D.), but the doctrine was expressly maintained by Augustine, and occurs in a Confession of Faith of an earlier Synod of Toledo (447 A.D.?), and in the words of Leo I. (Ep. ad Turib., c. 1), "de utroque processit." The addition was not embodied into the Creed as used at Rome as late as the beginning of the ninth century. (Vid. **Harnack,** Hist. of Dogma, iv. 132.) Prudentius probably followed, as regards the Trinity,

the doctrine generally held by the Spanish Church of his day; in many points it is difficult (cf. note on iii. 2), but appears to be derived partly from Tertullian and partly from Marcellus.

59   The identification of the Habakkuk of this legend (vid. the Apocryphal "Bel and the Dragon") with the O. T. prophet is erroneous. This version of the story of Daniel is sometimes represented in the frescoes of the Catacombs, where the subject is a very favourite one, as is natural in an age when the cry "Christiani ad leones" so often rang through the streets of Rome.

V

1   There has been much doubt as to the title and scope of this hymn. Some early editors (e.g., Fabricius and Arevalus) adopt the title "ad incensum cerei Paschalis," or "de novo lumine Paschalis Sabbati," and confine its object to the ceremonial of Easter Eve, which is specially alluded to in ll. 125 et seq. Others, following the best MSS., give the simpler title used in this text, and regard it as a hymn for daily use. This view is supported by the weight of evidence: the position of the hymn among the first six (none of which are for special days), and the fact that the Benediction of the Paschal Candle was not in use, at any rate in Rome, in the pontificate of Zacharias (ob. 752 A.D.) point in this direction. In the Spanish Church particularly the very ancient custom of praying at the hour when the evening lamps were lighted had developed into the regular office of the lucernarium, as distinct from Vespers. The Mozarabic Breviary (seventh century) contains the prayers and responses for this service, and the Rule of St. Isidore runs: "In the evening offices, first the lucernarium, then two psalms, one responsory and lauds, a hymn and prayer are to be said." St. Basil also writes: "It seemed good to our fathers not

to receive in silence the gift of the evening light, but to give thanks as soon as it appeared." It is probable, therefore, that Prudentius intended the hymn for daily use, and that after speaking of God as the source of light, and His manifestations in the form of fire to Moses and the Israelites, his thoughts pass naturally, though somewhat abruptly, to the special festival--Easter Eve--on which the sanctuaries were most brilliantly illuminated. The question is fully discussed by Brockhaus (A. Prudentius Clemens in seiner Bedeutung fuer die Kirche seiner Zeit), and Roesler (Der catholische Dichter A. Prudentius). Part of this hymn is used in the Mozarabic Breviary for the First Sunday after Epiphany, at Vespers, being stanzas 1, 7, 35, 38-41.

7   The words incussu silicis are perhaps reminiscent of the Spanish ceremonial of Easter Eve, when the bishop struck the flint, lighting from it first a candle, then a lamp, from which the deacons lighted their candles; these were blessed by the bishop, and the procession from the processus into the church followed.

21   Cf. Vaughan, The Lampe:--

    "Then thou dost weepe
Still as thou burn'st, and the warm droppings creepe
To measure out thy length."

119   The folium **here is probably the ancient** malobathrum, generally identified as the Indian cinnamon. The Arab traders who brought this valuable product into the Western markets, surrounded its origin with much mystery.

125   The following stanzas, in which Prudentius elaborates the beautiful fancy that the sufferings of lost spirits are alleviated at Eastertide, have incurred the severe censure of some of the

earlier editors. Fabricius calls it "a Spanish fabrication," while others, as Cardinal Bellarmine, declare that the author is speaking "poetically and not dogmatically." That such a belief, however, was actually held by some section of the ancient Church is evident from the words of St. Augustine (Encheiridion, c. 112): Paenas damnatorum certis temporum intervallis existiment, si hoc eis placet, aliquatenus mitigari, dummodo intelligatur in eis manere ira Dei, hoc est ipsa damnatio. "Let men believe, if it so please them, that at certain intervals the pains of the damned are somewhat alleviated, provided that it be understood that the wrath of God, that is damnation itself, abides upon them."

140   It is somewhat startling to find Prudentius speaking of the Holy Eucharist in terms which would recall to his contemporary readers Virgilian phraseology and the honeyed cake (liba) used in pagan sacrifice. It must be remembered, however, that in the early days of the Church paganism and Christianity flourished side by side for a considerable period; and we find various pagan practices allowed to continue, where they were innocent. Thus the bride-cake and the bridal-veil are of heathen origin; the mirth of the Saturnalia survives, in a modified form, in some of the rejoicings of Christmas; and the flowers, which had filled the pagan temples during the Floralia, were employed to adorn God's House at the Easter festival.

141   The brilliant illumination of churches on Easter Eve is very ancient. According to Eusebius, Constantine "turned the mystical vigil into the light of day by means of lamps suspended in every part, setting up also great waxen tapers, as large as columns, throughout the city." Gregory of Nyssa also speaks of "the cloud of fire mingling with the rays of the rising sun, and making the eve and the festival one continuous day without interval of darkness."

153   Cf. Paradise Lost, iii. 51:--

"So much the rather thou, Celestial Light,
Shine inward, and the mind through all her powers
Irradiate."

VI

The last seven stanzas of this hymn are used in the Moz. Brev. at
Compline on Passion Sunday, and daily until Maundy Thursday.

56   Cf. Job. vii. 14: "Then Thou scarest me with dreams, and terrifiest
me through visions."

95   In the translation of this stanza the explanation of Nebrissensis
is adopted, an early editor of Prudentius (1512) and one of the
leaders of the Renaissance in Spain. He considers that "the few of
the impious who are condemned to eternal death" are the incurable
sinners, immedicabiles. Others attempt to reconcile these words
with the general belief of the early Church by maintaining that
non pii *is not equivalent to* impii, but rather refers to the
class that is neither decidedly good nor definitely bad, and that
the mercy of God is extended to the majority of these. A third view
is that the poet is speaking relatively, and means that few are
condemned in proportion to the number that deserve condemnation.
In whatever way the words are explained, it is interesting to find
an advocate of "the larger hope" in the fourth century.

105   Cf. Rev. xvii. 8: "The beast that thou sawest was, and is not;
and is about to come up out of the abyss, and to go into perdition."

109   Cf. 2 Thess. ii. 4: "The son of perdition, who opposeth and
exalteth himself above all that is called God, or that is worshipped;
so that he as God sitteth in the temple of God, showing himself that

he is God."

127   The phrase rorem subisse sacrum would suggest baptism by
        sprinkling, except that Prudentius uses the word loosely elsewhere.
        Immersion was undoubtedly the general practice of the early Church,
        "clinical" baptism being allowed only in cases of necessity.

128   The anointing with oil showed that the catechumen was enrolled
        among the spiritual priesthood, and with the unction was joined the
        sign of the Cross on the forehead.

VII

1   This entire hymn is used in the Moz. Brev., divided into fifteen
      portions for use during Lent.

27   The word sacerdos here, as in ix. 4, is used in the sense of
        "prophet"; but in both passages there is some idea of the exercise
        of priestly functions. Elijah may be called "priest" from his having
        offered sacrifice on Mount Carmel, and David from his wearing the
        priestly ephod as he danced before the Ark.

69   The old editors discuss these lines with much gravity, and mostly
        come to the conclusion that "locusts" were "a kind of bird, of
        the length of a finger, with quick, short flight"; while the "wild
        honey" was not actual honey at all, but "the tender leaves of
        certain trees, which, when crushed by the fingers, had the pleasant
        savour of honey."

76   A gloss on one of the Vat. MSS. adds: "This is not authorised; for
        John merely baptized with water, and not in the name of the Father,
        Son and Holy Ghost; therefore his baptism was of no avail, save that

it prepared the way for Christ to baptize." Many of the Fathers, however, while expressly affirming that John's baptism differed from that of Christ, allowed that the stains of sin were washed away by the former. St. Chrysostom draws this distinction: "There was in John's baptism pardon, but not without repentance; remission of sins, but only attained by grief."

100   The story of Jonah, as a type of the Resurrection, is one of the most frequent subjects of the frescoes of the Catacombs. In one very ancient picture, a man in a small boat is depicted in the act of placing the prophet in the very jaws of the whale.

115   Two stanzas are omitted in the text, which depict the sufferings of Jonah with a wealth of detail not in accordance with modern taste. For the sake of giving a complete text, we append them here:--

> "Transmissa raptim praeda cassos dentium
> eludit ictus incruentam transvolans
> inpune linguam, ne retentam mordicus
> offam molares dissecarent uvidi,
> os omne transit et palatum praeterit.
>
> Ternis dierum ac noctium processibus
> mansit ferino devoratus gutture,
> errabat illic per latebras viscerum,
> ventris recessus circumibat tortiles
> anhelus extis intus aestuantibus."

194   Prudentius appears to have believed that the mystery of the Incarnation was concealed from Satan, and that the Temptation was an endeavour to ascertain whether Jesus was the Son of God or no. Cf. Milton, Par. Reg. i.:--

"Who this is we must learn, for Man he seems
In all his lineaments, though in his face
The glimpses of his Father's glory shine."

VIII

9   The day of twelve hours appears to have been adopted by the
Romans about B.C. 291. Ambrose (de virginibus, iii. 4), commenting
on Ps. cxix. and the words "Seven times a day do I praise thee,"
declares that prayers are to be offered up with thanksgiving when
we rise from sleep, when we go forth, when we prepare to take food,
when we have taken it, at the hour of incense, and lastly, when we
retire to rest. He probably alludes to private prayer. The stanza
here indicates that the second hour after midday has arrived, when
the fasting ended and the midday meal was taken.

14   The word festum, as in vii. 4, indicates a special fast day.
Until the sixth century, fasting was simply a penitential discipline
and was not used as a particular mode of penance. In the fourth
century it was a fairly common practice as a preparation for Holy
Communion. Fasting before Baptism was a much earlier practice.
The stated fasts of the Western Church were (1) annual, that
is, ante-paschal or Lent; (2) monthly, or the fasts of the four
seasons in the 1st, 4th, 7th and 10th months; (3) weekly, on
Wednesday and Friday. There was also the fast of the Rogations and
the Vigils or Eves of holy days. It is doubtful whether all these
were in vogue as early as Prudentius.

33   This passage on the Shepherd reminds us of one of the most common
pictorial representations of the Catacombs. Christian art owed
something to paganism in this matter; ancient sculptures represent

the god Pan with a goat thrown across his shoulders and a Pan's
pipe in his hand; while the poets Calpurnius and Tibullus both
refer to the custom of carrying a stray or neglected lamb on the
shoulders of the shepherd. Going further back, the figure is common
in the O. T. to express God's care over His people. Our Lord
therefore used for His own purpose and transfigured with new
meaning a familiar figure. The gradual transition from paganism
to Christianity is curiously illustrated by the fact that in several
of the Catacomb bas-reliefs and paintings the Good Shepherd holds in
His outstretched hand a Pan's pipe. See Maitland's *Church in the
Catacombs*, p. 315, for a woodcut of the Good Shepherd with a lamb
over His shoulders, two sheep at His feet, a palm tree (or poplar)
on either side, and a Pan's pipe in His right hand; and also the
frontispiece for a reproduction from the Cemetery of St. Peter and
St. Marcellinus.

IX

1   This hymn, which first introduced into sacred song the trochaic
metre familiar in Greek Tragedy and the Latin adaptations of it,
supplies the Moz. Brev. with some stanzas for use during Holy Week.
The lines selected are 22-24, 1-21.

11   The use of the symbol O, (pronounced here as a single
syllable), appears to indicate that the names Omega and Omikron
came into use at a later date than Prudentius' time. In Rev. i. 8,
the best MSS. read ego eimi to alpha kai to o.

33   The words vulnerum piamina are generally supposed to refer to
the "gifts which Moses commanded" to be offered by those healed of
leprosy (Lev. xiv. 2). If so, Prudentius' language may imply that
the cure was not actually complete until the offering of these gifts,

and is at variance with St. Matthew, viii. 43, "and forthwith his leprosy was cleansed." Probably, however, his idea is rather that the gifts to the priest formally marked the leper as a clean man.

71   Cf. note on iii. 199.

X

1   Parts of this hymn are used in the Moz. Brev. in the Office of the Dead, being ll. 1-16, 45-48, 57-68, 157-168.

The burial rites of the primitive Church were simple, and marked by an absence of the ostentatious expression of grief which the pagan peoples displayed. The general practice of cremation was rejected, partly owing to the new belief in the resurrection of the body, and partly from a desire to imitate the burial of the Lord. At Rome, during the first three centuries, the dead were laid in the Catacombs, in which Prudentius took conspicuous interest (see Translator's Note), but after 338 A.D. this practice became less frequent, and was completely abandoned after 410 A.D. Elsewhere, from the earliest times, the Christians purchased special enclosures (areae), which were often attacked and rifled by angry mobs in the days of persecution. The body was frequently embalmed (cf. ll. 51, 52), swathed in white linen (l. 49), and placed in a coffin; vigils and hymns continued for three or four days, but hired mourners were forbidden (l. 113), and instead of the dirges of the heathens, chants expressive of triumphant faith were sung as the body was carried to the grave, where a simple service was held, and evergreens and flowers were strewn about the tomb (ll. 169, 170). The earliest inscriptions are often roughly scratched on plaster, and consist merely of a name and age, or simple words like--

GEMELLA DORMIT IN PACE

but later (cf. l. 171), they were engraved on small marble slabs.

25   In both thought and language this stanza, as vii. 16 et seq., is
      evidently reminiscent of Horace (Sat. 2, ii. 77): Quin corpus
      onustum, etc.

> "The Body, too, with Yesterday's excess
> Burthened and tired, shall the pure Soul depress,
> Weigh down this Portion of celestial Birth,
> This Breath of God, and fix it to the Earth."
>   (Francis).

51   Boldetti, in his work on the Catacombs (lib. i. cap. 59), says
      that on many occasions, when he was present at the opening of a
      grave, the assembled company were conscious of a spicy odour
      diffusing itself from the tomb. Cf. Tertullian (Apol. 42): "The
      Arabs and Sabaeans knew well that we consume more of their precious
      merchandise for our dead than do the heathen for their gods."

57   Prudentius' firm faith in the resurrection of the body is also
      nobly expressed in the Apotheosis (ll. 1063 et seq.):--

> "Nosco meum in Christo corpus resurgere; quid me
> Desperare iubes? veniam, quibus ille revenit
> Calcata de morte viis: quod credimus hoc est.

> *   *   *   *   *

> Pellite corde metum, mea membra, et credite vosmet
> Cum Christo reditura Deo; nam vos gerit ille

Et secum revocat: morbos ridete minaces:
Inflictos casus contemnite; tetra sepulcra
Despuite; exsurgens quo Christus provocat, ite. "

Translation.

"I know in Christ my body shall arise;
Why bid me, then, despair? for I shall go
By that same path whereby my Lord returned,
Death trodden 'neath His feet: this is my creed.
Banish, my limbs, all terror; and believe
That ye with Christ our God shall yet return;
He beareth you and with Himself recalls.
Laugh at the threats of sickness; scorn the blows
Of fate; despise the horrors of the tomb;
And fare ye where the risen Christ doth call."

61   The poet expresses as a duty owed to Christ Himself the heathen
obligation of casting three handfuls of earth upon a body discovered
dead.

69   For the incident referred to in these lines, see the Apocryphal
book of Tobias, cc. ii. and xi. Tobit, a pious Israelite captive
in Nineveh, was reduced to beggary as the result of his zeal in
burying those of his countrymen who had been killed and exposed by
royal command. He also lost his sight, which was eventually restored
by the application of the gall of a fish which attacked his son
Tobias, and was killed by him. The "fish" of the legend is probably
the crocodile, whose gall was credited with medicinal properties by
various Greek and Latin writers. Cf. Pliny, N. H. xxviii. 8: "They
say that nothing avails more against cataract than to anoint the eyes
with its gall mixed with honey."

113   Cf. Cyprian (De Mortal. 20): "We must not lament our brethren whom the Lord's summons has freed from the world, for we know that they are not lost, but gone before. We may not wear the black robes of mourning while they have put on the white raiment of joy. Nor may we grieve for those as lost whom we know to be living with God."

171   Cf. Perist. vii.:--

"Nos pio fletu, date, perluamus
Marmorum sulcos."

The early Christian epitaphs, of which many thousands exist, are instinct with a faith which is in striking contrast to the unrelieved gloom or sullen resignation of paganism. We may compare with the common

AVE ATQVE VALE

"Hail and farewell"

or inscriptions like

INFANTI DVLCISSIMO QVEM DI IRATI AETERNO SOMNO DEDERUNT

"To a very sweet babe, whom the angry gods gave to unending sleep."

the Christian

DVLCIS ET INNOCENS HIC DORMIT SEVERIANVS SOMNO PACIS CVIVS

SPIRITVS IN LVCE DOMINI SVSCEPTVS EST (A.D. 393)

"Here slumbers in the sleep of peace the sweet and innocent Severianus, whose spirit is received in the light of the Lord"

or

NATVS EST LAVRENTIVS IN ETERNVM ANN. XX. DORMIT IN PACE (A.D. 329)

"Laurentius was born into eternity in his twentieth year. He sleeps in peace."

See also note on iii. 205.

XI

1   Virgil's Fourth Eclogue known as the "Pollio" has undoubtedly influenced the thought and style of this poem: the more noticeable parallels will be pointed out as they occur. In Milton's ode On the Morning of Christ's Nativity there are several passages which recall Prudentius' treatment of the theme in this and the succeeding hymn; but curiously enough, the Puritan poet in alluding to the season of the Nativity takes an opposite line of thought, and regards the diminished sunshine of winter as a veiling of an inferior flame before the light of "a greater Sun." Prudentius proclaims the increase of the sun's light, which begins after the winter solstice, as symbolic of the ever-widening influence of the True Light. The idea is given in a terse form by St. Peter Chrysologus, Serm. 159: Crescere dies coepit, quia verus dies illuxit. "The day begins to lengthen out, inasmuch as the true Day hath shone forth."

18   For the somewhat obscure phrase verbo editus, see note on iii. 2.

20   For "Sophia" or the Divine Creative Wisdom, see Prov. iii. 19, 20,
     and especially viii. 27-31, where the language "has been of signal
     importance in the history of thought, helping, as it does, to make
     a bridge between Eastern and Greek ideas, and to prepare the way
     for the Incarnation" (Davison, Wisdom-Literature of the O. T., pp.
     5, 6). In Alexandrian theology the conception of God's transcendence
     gave rise to the doctrine of an intermediate power or logos, by
     which creation was effected. In the Prologue of the fourth Gospel
     the idea was set forth in its purely Christian form. See 1, 3, where
     the Logos or the pre-incarnate Christ is described as the maker of
     all things--an idea which is also illustrated by the language of St.
     Paul in such passages as Col. i. 6.

59   Cf. for the conception of a golden age, Virg., Ecl., iv. 5
     et seq.: Magnus ab integro saeclorum nascitur ordo, etc.

65   Reminiscences of ancient prophecy appear to be embodied in this
     and following lines. Cf. Joel iii. 18: "And it shall come to pass
     in that day that the mountains shall drop down sweet wine and the
     hills shall flow with milk." Amos ix. 13: "The mountains shall drop
     sweet wine and all the hills shall melt." But cf. especially Virg.,
     Ecl., iv. 18-30: At tibi prima, puer, nullo munuscula cultu, etc.

     "Unbidden earth shall wreathing ivy bring,
     And fragrant herbs (the promises of spring)
     As her first off'rings to her infant king.

*   *   *   *   *

Unlaboured harvest shall the fields adorn,
And clustered grapes shall blush on every thorn;
The knotted oaks shall showers of honey weep,
And through the matted grass the liquid gold shall creep."
          (Dryden's Trans.)

81   The legend of the ox and ass adoring our Lord arose from an
allegorical interpretation of Isa. i. 3: "The ox knoweth his owner,
the ass his master's crib." Origen (Homilies on St. Luke xiii.)
is the first to allegorise on the passage in Isaiah, where the word
for "crib" in the Greek translation of the O. T. is identical with
St. Luke's word for "manger" (phatne). After referring to the
circumstances of the Nativity, Origen proceeds to say: "That was
what the prophet foretold, saying, 'The ox knoweth,' etc. The Ox is
a clean animal: the Ass an unclean one. The Ass knew his master's
crib (praesepe domini sui): not the people of Israel, but the
unclean animal out of pagan nations knew its master's crib. 'But
Israel hath not known me: and my people hath not understood.' Let us
understand this and press forward to the crib, recognise the Master
and be made worthy of his knowledge." The thought that the Ox = the
Jews and the Ass = Pagans, reappears in Gregory Nazianzen, Ambrose
and Jerome. See an interesting article by Mr. Austin West (Ox and
Ass Legend of the Nativity. Cont. Review, Dec. 1903), who notes
the further impetus given to the legend by the Latin rendering of
Habb. iii. 2 (LXX.) which in the Vetus Itala version appears as
"in medio duorum animalium in notesceris," "in the midst of two
animals shalt thou be known" (R.V., in the midst of the years make
it known). The legend does not appear in apocryphal Christian
literature earlier than in the Pseudo-Matthew Gospel, which

belongs to the later fifth century. It is interesting to note that
with St. Francis and the Franciscans the ox and the ass are merely
animals: the allegorical interpretation of Origen had vanished from
Christendom: and in its place we find St. Francis (see Life of St.
Francis by St. Bonaventura, "Temple Classics" edition, p. 111)
making a presepio at Greccio, to which a living ox and ass are
brought, in order that a visible representation of the manger-scene
might kindle the devotion of the Brethren and the assembled
townsfolk. This act of St. Francis inaugurated the custom, still
observed in the Roman Church, of representing by means of waxen
images the whole of the Nativity manger-scene, Mother and Child
together with the adoring animals.

97   For the obstetrix, cf. Proto-Evangelium of the Pseudo-James (a
      Greek romance of the fourth century), Sec. 18 et seq., where Joseph
      is represented as seeking and finding a Hebrew midwife.

100   Cf. Milton's Ode on the Nativity, ll. 157-164:--

      "With such a horrid clang
      As on Mount Sinai rang
        While the red fire and smould'ring clouds outbrake:
      The aged earth aghast
      With terror of that blast,
        Shall from the surface to the centre shake;
      When at the world's last session
      The dreadful Judge in middle air shall spread his throne."

XII

1   This poem has given four hymns to the Roman Breviary:--
(1) For the Feast of the Transfiguration, Vespers and Matins
consisting of ll. 1-4, 37-40, 41-44, 85-88.
(2) For the Epiphany at Lauds, beginning O sola magnarum urbium,
ll. 77-80, 5-8, 61-72.
(3) For the Feast of Holy Innocents at Matins, beginning Audit
tyrannus anxius, ll. 93-100, 133-136.
(4) Also the Feast of Holy Innocents at Lauds, beginning Salvete
flores martyrum, ll. 125-132.

5   For a curious parallel to these opening lines see Henry Vaughan's
Pious Thoughts and Ejaculations (the Nativity):--

> "But stay! what light is that doth stream
> And drop here in a gilded beam?
> It is Thy star runs Page and brings
> Thy tributary Eastern kings.
> Lord! grant some light to us that we
> May find with them the way to Thee!"

12   Cf. Ignatius, Ep. ad Ephes. xix.: "All the other stars, together
with the Sun and Moon, became a chorus to the Star, which in its
light excelled them all."

15   Prudentius mentions the constellations of Ursa Major and Ursa
Minor (to which latter the Pole Star belongs) as examples of stars
in constant apparition. All the Little Bear stars are within about
24 deg. from the Pole; hence, if viewed from Saragossa, the birthplace
of Prudentius, the lowest altitude of any of them would be 18 deg.

above the north horizon. The same applies to the majority of the stars in the Great Bear. Some few would sink below the horizon for a brief time in each twenty-four hours; but the greater number, especially the seven principal stars known as the "Plough," would be sufficiently high up at their lowest northern altitudes to be in perpetual apparition. [My friend, Rev. R. Killip, F.R.A.S., has kindly furnished me with these particulars.] Allusions to the Bears are constantly recurring in the classical poets (cf. e.g. Ovid., Met. *xiii. 293,* immunemque aequoris Arcton, "the Bear that never touches the sea"). The idea that these stars are mostly hidden by clouds, though perpetually in view, is a poetic hyperbole intended to enhance the uniqueness of the Star of Bethlehem.

49 ․ Jerome (ad Eustoch. Ep. 22) commenting on the passage in Isa. xi. 1, "And there shall come forth a rod out of the root of Jesse, and a flower shall rise up out of his root" (Vulg.), remarks: "The rod (virga) is the mother of the Lord, simple, pure, sincere ... the flower of the rod is Christ, who saith, 'I am the flower of the field and the lily of the valleys.'"

69   This symbolism of the gifts of the Magi is also found in Juvencus (I. 250): "Frankincense, gold and myrrh they bring as gifts to a King, a Man and a God," and is again alluded to by Prudentius in Apoth. *631* et seq. The idea is expressed in the hymn of Jacopone da Todi, beginning Verbum caro factum est (Mone, Hymni Latini, Vol. 2):

> "Gold to the kingly,
> Incense to the priestly,
> Myrrh to the mortal:"

and it has passed into the Office for Epiphany in the Roman Breviary: "There are three precious gifts which the Magi offered to their Lord that day, and they contain in themselves sacred mysteries: in the gold, that the power of a king may be displayed: in the frankincense, consider the great high priest: in the myrrh, the burial of the Lord" et passim.

172   The idea that Moses defeated the Amalekites because his arms were outstretched in the form of a cross is found also in one of the hymns (lxi.) of Gregory Nazianzen. The symbol of the Christian religion, the cross, "was fancifully traced by the Fathers throughout the universe: the four points of the compass, the 'height, breadth, length and depth' of the Apostle expressed, or were expressed by, the cross.... The cross explained everything" (Maitland, Church in the Catacombs, p. 202).

193   The discomfiture of the heathen gods wrought by the Incarnation is elaborated by Milton, whose lines recall this and similar passages in Prudentius:--

"Peor, and Baaelim
Forsake their temples dim

     *   *   *   *   *

And sullen Moloch fled,
Hath left in shadows dread,
  His burning idol all of blackest hue.

Our Babe, to show his Godhead true,
Can in his swaddling bands control the damned crew."

The Codes Of Hammurabi And Moses
W. W. Davies

QTY

The discovery of the Hammurabi Code is one of the greatest achievements of archaeology, and is of paramount interest, not only to the student of the Bible, but also to all those interested in ancient history...

Religion   **ISBN:** *1-59462-338-4*   **Pages:132**
MSRP $12.95

The Theory of Moral Sentiments
Adam Smith

QTY

This work from 1749. contains original theories of conscience amd moral judgment and it is the foundation for systemof morals.

Philosophy   **ISBN:** *1-59462-777-0*   **Pages:536**
MSRP $19.95

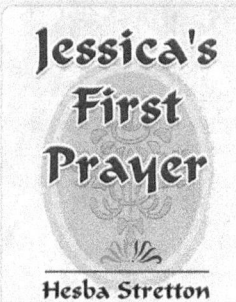

Jessica's First Prayer
Hesba Stretton

QTY

In a screened and secluded corner of one of the many railway-bridges which span the streets of London there could be seen a few years ago, from five o'clock every morning until half past eight, a tidily set-out coffee-stall, consisting of a trestle and board, upon which stood two large tin cans, with a small fire of charcoal burning under each so as to keep the coffee boiling during the early hours of the morning when the work-people were thronging into the city on their way to their daily toil...

Pages:84

Childrens   **ISBN:** *1-59462-373-2*   *MSRP $9.95*

My Life and Work
Henry Ford

QTY

Henry Ford revolutionized the world with his implementation of mass production for the Model T automobile. Gain valuable business insight into his life and work with his own auto-biography... "We have only started on our development of our country we have not as yet, with all our talk of wonderful progress, done more than scratch the surface. The progress has been wonderful enough but..."

Pages:300

Biographies/   **ISBN:** *1-59462-198-5*   *MSRP $21.95*

The Art of Cross-Examination
Francis Wellman

QTY

I presume it is the experience of every author, after his first book is published upon an important subject, to be almost overwhelmed with a wealth of ideas and illustrations which could readily have been included in his book, and which to his own mind, at least, seem to make a second edition inevitable. Such certainly was the case with me; and when the first edition had reached its sixth impression in five months, I rejoiced to learn that it seemed to my publishers that the book had met with a sufficiently favorable reception to justify a second and considerably enlarged edition. ..

Pages:412

Reference   **ISBN:** *1-59462-647-2*   *MSRP $19.95*

On the Duty of Civil Disobedience
Henry David Thoreau

QTY

Thoreau wrote his famous essay, On the Duty of Civil Disobedience, as a protest against an unjust but popular war and the immoral but popular institution of slave-owning. He did more than write—he declined to pay his taxes, and was hauled off to gaol in consequence. Who can say how much this refusal of his hastened the end of the war and of slavery ?

Law   **ISBN:** *1-59462-747-9*   **Pages:48**

MSRP $7.45

Dream Psychology Psychoanalysis for Beginners
Sigmund Freud

QTY

Sigmund Freud, born Sigismund Schlomo Freud (May 6, 1856 - September 23, 1939), was a Jewish-Austrian neurologist and psychiatrist who co-founded the psychoanalytic school of psychology. Freud is best known for his theories of the unconscious mind, especially involving the mechanism of repression; his redefinition of sexual desire as mobile and directed towards a wide variety of objects; and his therapeutic techniques, especially his understanding of transference in the therapeutic relationship and the presumed value of dreams as sources of insight into unconscious desires.

Pages:196

Psychology   **ISBN:** *1-59462-905-6*   *MSRP $15.45*

The Miracle of Right Thought
Orison Swett Marden

QTY

Believe with all of your heart that you will do what you were made to do. When the mind has once formed the habit of holding cheerful, happy, prosperous pictures, it will not be easy to form the opposite habit. It does not matter how improbable or how far away this realization may see, or how dark the prospects may be, if we visualize them as best we can, as vividly as possible, hold tenaciously to them and vigorously struggle to attain them, they will gradually become actualized, realized in the life. But a desire, a longing without endeavor, a yearning abandoned or held indifferently will vanish without realization.

Pages:360

Self Help   **ISBN:** *1-59462-644-8*   *MSRP $25.45*

www.bookjungle.com *email: sales@bookjungle.com fax: 630-214-0564 mail: Book Jungle PO Box 2226 Champaign, IL 61825*

QTY

The Rosicrucian Cosmo-Conception Mystic Christianity *by Max Heindel*   ISBN: *1-59462-188-8*   **$38.95**
The Rosicrucian Cosmo-conception is not dogmatic, neither does it appeal to any other authority than the reason of the student. It is: not controversial, but is: sent forth in the, hope that it may help to clear...   *New Age/Religion Pages 646*

Abandonment To Divine Providence *by Jean-Pierre de Caussade*   ISBN: *1-59462-228-0*   **$25.95**
"The Rev. Jean Pierre de Caussade was one of the most remarkable spiritual writers of the Society of Jesus in France in the 18th Century. His death took place at Toulouse in 1751. His works have gone through many editions and have been republished...   *Inspirational/Religion Pages 400*

Mental Chemistry *by Charles Haanel*   ISBN: *1-59462-192-6*   **$23.95**
Mental Chemistry allows the change of material conditions by combining and appropriately utilizing the power of the mind. Much like applied chemistry creates something new and unique out of careful combinations of chemicals the mastery of mental chemistry...   *New Age Pages 354*

The Letters of Robert Browning and Elizabeth Barret Barrett 1845-1846 vol II   ISBN: *1-59462-193-4*   **$35.95**
by Robert Browning and Elizabeth Barrett   *Biographies Pages 596*

Gleanings In Genesis (volume I) *by Arthur W. Pink*   ISBN: *1-59462-130-6*   **$27.45**
Appropriately has Genesis been termed "the seed plot of the Bible" for in it we have, in germ form, almost all of the great doctrines which are afterwards fully developed in the books of Scripture which follow...   *Religion/Inspirational Pages 420*

The Master Key *by L. W. de Laurence*   ISBN: *1-59462-001-6*   **$30.95**
In no branch of human knowledge has there been a more lively increase of the spirit of research during the past few years than in the study of Psychology, Concentration and Mental Discipline. The requests for authentic lessons in Thought Control, Mental Discipline and...   *New Age/Business Pages 422*

The Lesser Key Of Solomon Goetia *by L. W. de Laurence*   ISBN: *1-59462-092-X*   **$9.95**
This translation of the first book of the "Lernegton" which is now for the first time made accessible to students of Talismanic Magic was done, after careful collation and edition, from numerous Ancient Manuscripts in Hebrew, Latin, and French...   *New Age/Occult Pages 92*

Rubaiyat Of Omar Khayyam *by Edward Fitzgerald*   ISBN:*1-59462-332-5*   **$13.95**
Edward Fitzgerald, whom the world has already learned, in spite of his own efforts to remain within the shadow of anonymity, to look upon as one of the rarest poets of the century, was born at Bredfield, in Suffolk, on the 31st of March, 1809. He was the third son of John Purcell...   *Music Pages 172*

Ancient Law *by Henry Maine*   ISBN: *1-59462-128-4*   **$29.95**
The chief object of the following pages is to indicate some of the earliest ideas of mankind, as they are reflected in Ancient Law, and to point out the relation of those ideas to modern thought.   *Religion/History Pages 152*

Far-Away Stories *by William J. Locke*   ISBN: *1-59462-129-2*   **$19.45**
"Good wine needs no bush, but a collection of mixed vintages does. And this book is just such a collection. Some of the stories I do not want to remain buried for ever in the museum files of dead magazine-numbers an author's not unpardonable vanity..."   *Fiction Pages 272*

Life of David Crockett *by David Crockett*   ISBN: *1-59462-250-7*   **$27.45**
"Colonel David Crockett was one of the most remarkable men of the times in which he lived. Born in humble life, but gifted with a strong will, an indomitable courage, and unremitting perseverance...   *Biographies/New Age Pages 424*

Lip-Reading *by Edward Nitchie*   ISBN: *1-59462-206-X*   **$25.95**
Edward B. Nitchie, founder of the New York School for the Hard of Hearing, now the Nitchie School of Lip-Reading, Inc, wrote "LIP-READING Principles and Practice". The development and perfecting of this meritorious work on lip-reading was an undertaking...   *How-to Pages 400*

A Handbook of Suggestive Therapeutics, Applied Hypnotism, Psychic Science   ISBN: *1-59462-214-0*   **$24.95**
by Henry Munro   *Health/New Age/Health/Self-help Pages 376*

A Doll's House: and Two Other Plays *by Henrik Ibsen*   ISBN: *1-59462-112-8*   **$19.95**
Henrik Ibsen created this classic when in revolutionary 1848 Rome. Introducing some striking concepts in playwriting for the realist genre, this play has been studied the world over.   *Fiction/Classics/Plays 308*

The Light of Asia *by sir Edwin Arnold*   ISBN: *1-59462-204-3*   **$13.95**
In this poetic masterpiece, Edwin Arnold describes the life and teachings of Buddha. The man who was to become known as Buddha to the world was born as Prince Gautama of India but he rejected the worldly riches and abandoned the reigns of power when...   *Religion/History/Biographies Pages 170*

The Complete Works of Guy de Maupassant *by Guy de Maupassant*   ISBN: *1-59462-157-8*   **$16.95**
"For days and days, nights and nights, I had dreamed of that first kiss which was to consecrate our engagement, and I knew not on what spot I should put my lips..."   *Fiction/Classics Pages 240*

The Art of Cross-Examination *by Francis L. Wellman*   ISBN: *1-59462-309-0*   **$26.95**
Written by a renowned trial lawyer, Wellman imparts his experience and uses case studies to explain how to use psychology to extract desired information through questioning.   *How-to/Science/Reference Pages 408*

Answered or Unanswered? *by Louisa Vaughan*   ISBN: *1-59462-248-5*   **$10.95**
Miracles of Faith in China   *Religion Pages 112*

The Edinburgh Lectures on Mental Science (1909) *by Thomas*   ISBN: *1-59462-008-3*   **$11.95**
This book contains the substance of a course of lectures recently given by the writer in the Queen Street Hall, Edinburgh. Its purpose is to indicate the Natural Principles governing the relation between Mental Action and Material Conditions...   *New Age/Psychology Pages 148*

Ayesha *by H. Rider Haggard*   ISBN: *1-59462-301-5*   **$24.95**
Verily and indeed it is the unexpected that happens! Probably if there was one person upon the earth from whom the Editor of this, and of a certain previous history, did not expect to hear again...   *Classics Pages 380*

Ayala's Angel *by Anthony Trollope*   ISBN: *1-59462-352-X*   **$29.95**
The two girls were both pretty, but Lucy who was twenty-one who supposed to be simple and comparatively unattractive, whereas Ayala was credited, as her Bombwhat romantic name might show, with poetic charm and a taste for romance. Ayala when her father died was nineteen...   *Fiction Pages 484*

The American Commonwealth *by James Bryce*   ISBN: *1-59462-286-8*   **$34.45**
An interpretation of American democratic political theory. It examines political mechanics and society from the perspective of Scotsman James Bryce   *Politics Pages 572*

Stories of the Pilgrims *by Margaret P. Pumphrey*   ISBN: *1-59462-116-0*   **$17.95**
This book explores pilgrims religious oppression in England as well as their escape to Holland and eventual crossing to America on the Mayflower, and their early days in New England...   *History Pages 268*

www.bookjungle.com *email: sales@bookjungle.com fax: 630-214-0564 mail: Book Jungle PO Box 2226 Champaign, IL 61825*

QTY

The Fasting Cure *by Sinclair Upton*   ISBN: *1-59462-222-1*   **$13.95**

In the Cosmopolitan Magazine for May, 1910, and in the Contemporary Review (London) for April, 1910, I published an article dealing with my experiences in fasting. I have written a great many magazine articles, but never one which attracted so much attention... New Age/Self Help/Health Pages 164

Hebrew Astrology *by Sepharial*   ISBN: *1-59462-308-2*   **$13.45**

In these days of advanced thinking it is a matter of common observation that we have left many of the old landmarks behind and that we are now pressing forward to greater heights and to a wider horizon than that which represented the mind-content of our progenitors... Astrology Pages 144

Thought Vibration or The Law of Attraction in the Thought World   ISBN: *1-59462-127-6*   **$12.95**

by William Walker Atkinson   *Psychology/Religion Pages 144*

Optimism *by Helen Keller*   ISBN: *1-59462-108-X*   **$15.95**

Helen Keller was blind, deaf, and mute since 19 months old, yet famously learned how to overcome these handicaps, communicate with the world, and spread her lectures promoting optimism. An inspiring read for everyone... Biographies/Inspirational Pages 84

Sara Crewe *by Frances Burnett*   ISBN: *1-59462-360-0*   **$9.45**

In the first place, Miss Minchin lived in London. Her home was a large, dull, tall one, in a large, dull square, where all the houses were alike, and all the sparrows were alike, and where all the door-knockers made the same heavy sound... Childrens/Classic Pages 88

The Autobiography of Benjamin Franklin *by Benjamin Franklin*   ISBN: *1-59462-135-7*   **$24.95**

The Autobiography of Benjamin Franklin has probably been more extensively read than any other American historical work, and no other book of its kind has had such ups and downs of fortune. Franklin lived for many years in England, where he was agent... Biographies/History Pages 332

Name	
Email	
Telephone	
Address	
City, State ZIP	

☐ **Credit Card**   ☐ **Check / Money Order**

Credit Card Number	
Expiration Date	
Signature	

Please Mail to: Book Jungle
                    PO Box 2226
                    Champaign, IL 61825
or Fax to: 630-214-0564

ORDERING INFORMATION

web: *www.bookjungle.com*
email: *sales@bookjungle.com*
fax: *630-214-0564*
mail: *Book Jungle PO Box 2226 Champaign, IL 61825*
or PayPal *to sales@bookjungle.com*

Please contact us for bulk discounts

DIRECT-ORDER TERMS

**20% Discount if You Order
Two or More Books**
Free Domestic Shipping!
Accepted: Master Card, Visa,
Discover, American Express

www.ingramcontent.com/pod-product-compliance
Lightning Source LLC
Chambersburg PA
CBHW080728020726

47503CB00010B/2830